A GAMBLE WITH HEARTS

Quintus Tiverton's handsome face was marred by an angry scowl.

Granted he had saved Selina from a most unsavory predicament, but now he was forced to look after the girl. Quintus was on his way to fashionable Baden-Baden, pursuing his livelihood at the gaming tables.

The casinos were no place for Selina. Her beauty would only prove a costly distraction. Her reputation would suffer from exposure to the spa's more disreputable patrons.

Quintus resigned himself to the inconvenience. After all, Selina had given him her word of honor that she would accept the first suitable offer of marriage.

It was a promise his lovely traveling companion would live to regret.

BARBARA CARTLAND

Bantam Books by Barbara Cartland
Ask your bookseller for the books you have missed

Barbara Cartland

A GAMBLE
WITH HEARTS

BANTAM BOOKS
TORONTO · NEW YORK · LONDON

A GAMBLE WITH HEARTS
A Bantam Book / February 1976

Published simultaneously in the United States and Canada

Bantam Books are published by Bantam Books, Inc. Its trade-
mark, consisting of the words "Bantam Books" and the por-
trayal of a bantam, is registered in the United States Patent
Office and in other countries. Marca Registrada. Bantam
Books, Inc., 666 Fifth Avenue, New York, New York 10019.

Author's Note

Baden, "The Pearl of the Black Forest" in the 1860s, was the summer capital of Europe. The description of the visitors to this enchanted town is accurate.

"Madame Maximus"—Léonide Leblanc—was there with the Royal Duc d'Aumale, and she twice broke the bank in the Casino.

In 1868 Caroline Letessier was forced to leave St. Petersburg and the Grand Duke left with her.

They settled in a sumptuous Villa just off the Lichtenthal Strasse, and the incident in the Casino with Hortense Schneider is authentic.

When Léonide Leblanc died of cancer at the age of fifty-two, Dumas *fils* said jokingly: "She will have a national funeral and the Duc d'Aumale will command the troops."

Caroline Letessier saved nothing of her fortune and died ugly and forgotten in absolute poverty.

Chapter One
1868

It was pouring with rain and bitterly cold with the wind blowing from the mountains as a gentleman rode into the court-yard of the Posting Inn.

The lighted windows, the chatter of voices, and the sound of laughter were welcoming after a long ride in which the elements had been more unpleasant than the mud and roughness of the road.

The gentleman swung himself down from the saddle and waited while his servant on another horse came forward to take the bridle, then he walked into the Inn.

He was surprised to find as he entered through the door quite an inordinate number of people grouped about a log fire in a low-ceilinged room, drinking and smoking.

He walked to where the Landlord was busy pouring beer into pewter mugs to say in a tone of authority:

"I want a bed-chamber for the night for myself and one for my servant."

"Impossible, *Mein Herr*," the Landlord replied without raising his eyes.

Then, as if under some compulsion, he looked up and, noting the appearance of the traveller, said in a very different tone:

"It is with the deepest regret, *Mein Herr*, that I cannot accommodate you, but the fact is, we have more guests than we can cope with as it is."

The gentleman looked round him.

"Where have they all come from?" he asked curiously.

He was well aware that this was only a minor Posting Inn, so he had certainly not expected to find it filled

1

with elegant ladies in silk gowns and expensive furs, or gentlemen wearing fashionably cut, tight-fitting jackets and sable-lined overcoats.

"There has been a fall of stone on the railway line, *Mein Herr*. These travellers are all on their way to Baden-Baden and have preferred to seek shelter in my Inn rather than spend the night in the train."

"I presume you can provide me with a meal of sorts?" the gentleman asked.

"Indeed, *Mein Herr*, it will be a pleasure, and I can only offer you my sincere regrets that we have no bedchamber available."

As the Landlord spoke, his wife, a portly woman wearing a mob-cap and a white apron, came to his side and whispered something in his ear.

The Inn-keeper appeared to hesitate and then he said:

"I hardly dare suggest it, *Mein Herr*, but there is an attic-room still unoccupied. It is one which is usually alloted to a servant; but at least you could lie down, and it would be more pleasant than spending the night in a chair."

"I will take it!" the stranger said briefly. "And now, if someone will wait upon me in the Dining-Hall, I wish to order some wine."

He strode away in what was obviously the direction of the Dining-Hall, and the Inn-keeper's wife's eyes followed him admiringly.

There was no doubt that he was not only handsome but distinguished in appearance, and his clothes, she noted, were worn with the indifferent elegance which proclaimed him an Englishman.

Like her husband, she had not failed to notice the gold signet ring on his finger, or the pearl pin in his cravat.

It was not only the impression of wealth and elegance which made her eyes follow the gentleman until he was out of sight; there was something else about him; something which had made several women, as he passed through the crowded room, look at him and look again.

As it was late, the Dining-Hall was empty save for a couple of elderly men lingering over a bottle of port.

The new arrival seated himself at a table near the open fireplace. When the waiter came hurrying to take his order, he scrutinised the menu with care, selecting his dishes with a fastidiousness and knowledge of food which ensured him more respect than was accorded to most travellers.

Finally, after a short wait, he was provided with well-cooked pike, a tender fowl, venison marinated in wine, a choice of Zuckerwerk or Pffanmenmus, and a selection of fruit dishes which were all appetising.

The wine was not exceptional but certainly drinkable, and when he had eaten amply—for it was his first meal of the day—the gentleman sat back in his chair and sipped his port.

He was warm; he was no longer hungry; and whatever the bed that awaited him upstairs was like, he knew that he would sleep well.

The Dining-Hall was now empty and the room which had been filled with travellers when he passed through it was much quieter.

Most of the women had retired upstairs to the bed-chambers allotted to them, and the men, who were left still smoking round the fireside, were nodding their heads, obviously too tired to talk.

The gentleman looked round for the Landlord and found him totting up his accounts of the drink that had been consumed.

"My bed-room is ready for me?" the gentleman asked.

"Your servant has taken up your things, *Mein Herr*, and I can only once again express my regrets that I cannot offer you a more worthy place for your slumbers."

"I daresay I shall fare all right," the stranger said genially.

"If you will climb the stairs, *Mein Herr*, the room is in the attics, the first door you come to as you reach the top landing."

"I will find it," the gentleman answered, and strolled slowly up the uncarpeted oak staircase which twisted and turned until finally he reached the attics, which were so low-ceilinged that he had to bend his head.

He was well aware that the attic-rooms in such an Inn, being immediately under the roof, would be hot in summer and cold in winter, and it was with a feeling of relief as he opened the door that he saw a light in the fireplace and realised that his servant had lit a fire.

It was smoking a little, which was not surprising, as it was unlikely that the chimney would have been used very often by those who could afford only such poor and austere accommodation.

The room was small and contained a bed which stood against one wall, and a chair.

The bed had obviously seen better days and must have been moved from one of the better rooms in the Inn into the attics in order to dispose of it.

It was a high, unwieldy box-bed beloved of the German *Hausfrau,* and the curtains which had once ensured privacy were now threadbare and full of holes.

But at a glance the gentleman could see that the coarse linen sheets were clean, and he was quite certain that the mattress would be of goose-feathers and therefore extremely comfortable.

He lit a candle which stood on the mantelshelf from a taper which he kindled from the flames of the fire, and as he did so he heard a scream.

It came from the room next door, and as he stood still to listen there was another scream, and yet another.

As they were low-pitched the gentleman walked across the room to stand near the opposite wall, so that he could hear what was happening.

To his astonishment, he heard a woman's voice say in English:

"No ... no ... please do not ... hit me any more ... I am ... sorry, I tell you ... I am ... sorry ... I did not ... mean to do it."

"Whether you meant it or not, you know what you have done, and I will make certain that you never do such a thing again," another woman's voice replied viciously.

There was the sound of a whip being applied forcefully and each sharp crack brought forth another half-stifled scream. Again a voice pleaded:

"P-please . . . please . . . no more . . . I could not . . . help it . . . I swear . . . I could . . . not help . . . it."

The noise of the whip was almost monotonous, until the screams became weaker.

"Let this be a lesson to you," the woman's voice said sharply, "a lesson you will not forget. When we reach Baden-Baden, you will obey me and do what I wish, otherwise I will hand you over to the police, and they will send you back to Paris to face the guillotine. Is that clear?"

There was no answer and the woman went on with a venomous note in her voice:

"You will obey me and do exactly what I say! Otherwise the beating I have given you tonight will be child's play to what you will receive. Think about it, Selina—just think about it."

There was the sound of someone moving across the uncarpeted floor. Then the door of the attic-room next to the gentleman's closed with a slam and he heard footsteps descending the stairs.

He was just about to return to the comfort of the fire when he heard the sound of tempestuous weeping, so agonising that it sounded as if whoever was crying had lost the last vestige of self-control.

The gentleman listened for a moment, then resolutely moved across the room.

"It is none of my business," he told himself.

But the sound of weeping was inescapable: even at the furthest end of his room he could still hear it, and he knew that he would be unable to sleep so long as it continued.

For a moment he seemed to debate with himself. Then he took the candle from the mantelshelf and opening his door went out onto the landing.

He walked a few steps until he came to the next room.

In the lock he could see a key and realised that when the woman had gone downstairs she had turned it. Whoever was weeping was locked in.

Again the gentleman hesitated for a moment, and then he knocked gently on the door.

The weeping ceased. There was a sudden silence. He knocked again.

There was no answer and after a second he turned the key and entered the room.

The attic was almost identical to his own except for the fact that there was no fire. There was one candle on a deal-table beside the bed.

The gentleman stood just inside the door, and by the light of his own candle and that on the table he could see a recumbent figure lying on top of the bed.

At first he thought it was a child. Then a face was raised from the pillow and he found himself looking at two very large, tear-filled eyes in a small, heart-shaped face.

Tears were running down a girl's pale cheeks and her fair hair fell over her shoulders.

"W-what . . . do you . . . want?"

There was no doubt of the terror in her voice and the gentleman said gently:

"Do not be afraid. I came only to see if I could help you."

The girl on the bed drew in her breath and the tears in her eyes spilled over as she answered brokenly:

"No-one can . . . help me."

"Are you sure of that?" the gentleman asked.

"Q-quite . . . sure," she answered, and her voice broke on the words.

The gentleman paused for a moment and then said:

"As one English person to another in a foreign country, I think perhaps we might discuss your problem."

He thought he saw an expression of hope in her face before she answered:

"You . . . you are . . . very kind . . . but you . . . cannot help me . . . it is . . . impossible!"

The gentleman smiled.

"I have a strange antipathy to being told that any problem is impossible. I have always believed that every difficulty is surmountable if one goes the right way about it."

The girl's eyes were on his face and he had the feeling that she was wondering if she could trust him.

"I promise you," he said in a quiet voice, "that if you wish me to leave you alone, I will do so. But if you continue to cry as wretchedly as you have been doing, I shall find it impossible to sleep on the other side of the wall."

"You . . . heard what . . . happened?" the girl asked in a low voice.

"I heard," he answered.

"There is no . . . reason why I should . . . burden you with my . . . problem."

"As I have just said, we are fellow-countrymen, and I am also extremely curious as to why you should be so cruelly treated."

He glanced at her body as he spoke and she made a little nervous gesture of modesty.

She was wearing only a thin cotton night-gown, buttoned at the neck and with long sleeves. In the light from the candles it was easy to see the spots of blood from the weals raised on her back by the whip.

"Suppose," the gentleman suggested in a calm, matter-of-fact voice, "you get under the bed-clothes where you will be warmer. I will turn my back while you do so, and then you can tell me what you have done to incur such punishment."

As he spoke he moved across the room to place his candle on the narrow mantelshelf over the empty grate.

The shutters were fastened over the window, but even so the room was cold and he thought with regret of the fire burning warmly next door in his own bedroom.

There was the sound of a movement behind him and then a low, still-frightened little voice said:

"I . . . I am . . . in bed."

He turned round.

She was sitting up, a sheet held against her chest. Her fair hair fell over her shoulders, making her look as if she had stepped from a fairy-story.

The gentleman moved towards her, looking as he did so to see if there was a chair on which he could sit. The only one in the attic was covered with the girl's clothes, and when he reached the bed he sat down on the extreme end of it.

"Now tell me," he said, "why you are here."

As he spoke he looked at her and realised that even with a tear-stained face she was unusually lovely. In fact, he told himself, he had not seen anyone so beautiful for a long time.

Her skin was almost translucent; her eyes were the deep blue of the Mediterranean, or perhaps of the gentians which could be picked high above them on the mountainside.

Her nose was very small and straight; her lips, still trembling, although smudged a little with the agony of her tears, were exquisitely curved.

"Who are you?" the gentleman asked.

"My name is . . . Selina Wade."

"And mine is Quintus Tiverton. So now we are introduced."

He smiled as he spoke, and it was a very beguiling smile, as women had found since he first used it to his advantage when he was in the cradle.

"D-do you . . . really want me to . . . tell you about . . . myself?" Selina asked hesitatingly.

"I must beg you to do so," Quintus Tiverton replied, "otherwise I assure you I shall lie awake all night worrying as to what is the truth."

"Y-you . . . will be . . . shocked when you . . . hear."

There was a smile at the corners of his lips as he answered:

"I can assure you, Miss Wade, nothing ever shocks me."

Selina gave a little sigh and leant back against the pillows.

It was an involuntary gesture and the weals on her back caused her to wince so that she sat up again.

"How could anyone dare to treat you in such a way?" Quintus Tiverton asked sharply.

"I . . . I suppose it was my own . . . fault," Selina replied. "But there was . . . nothing else I could . . . do . . . really there was not!"

"I believe you," Quintus Tiverton said. "But you must tell me first what I am to believe."

He smiled again and realised that Selina, who had been trembling ever since he entered the room, now seemed a little calmer.

"It is all . . . so . . . bewildering. When Mrs. Devilin asked me to go with her to . . . France, I thought it would be . . . exciting and an . . . adventure, but it has been . . . terrifying!"

"Who is Mrs. Devilin?" Quintus Tiverton enquired.

"I met her in the . . . Domestic Bureau," Selina replied.

"Start at the beginning," Quintus Tiverton said. "Who are your parents and where do you live?"

"My parents both are dead," Selina answered. "We lived at Little Cobham in Surrey."

"I know it," Quintus Tiverton said. "What did your father do?"

"He had a small Estate," Selina replied, "which he bought after he retired from the Army. He was a Colonel in the Eleventh Hussars."

The man listening to her did not speak, and after a moment she went on:

"He had his pension, and Mama had a little money of her own. But when Papa died and his pension stopped I found Mama's capital had all been spent, and so there was . . . nothing."

"The house did not belong to you?"

"I thought it did, but it was mortgaged."

Selina gave a little sigh.

"I had always imagined that I would go on living at home if anything happened to Papa. I could have arranged for some respectable woman to live with me . . . but then I learnt that the house was no longer mine."

There was something pathetically lost and child-like in the way she said it and after a moment Quintus Tiverton prompted:

"What happened?"

"My Uncle told me I could live with him, but he obviously did not really want me. He is a Parson living on a very small stipend and it is hard enough for him to make two ends meet."

She made a little gesture with her hand as she said:

"When I suggested to my Uncle that I should find work he seemed pleased. So I went to London."

"By yourself?" Quintus Tiverton asked.

"There was no-one to go with me," Selina replied, "and Uncle Bartram was too busy to spare the time."

"I understand. Go on."

"I knew, of course, I would have to go to a Domestic Bureau," Selina continued. "I thought they would advise me as to what sort of employment I should take. I . . . I am afraid . . . I am not very . . . talented."

Looking at her face, at her big eyes raised to his, Quintus Tiverton could not help thinking that there would be no need for a girl of such beauty to possess many talents.

But he made no comment, anxious for Selina to continue her story.

"I had only just begun to explain to the Secretary at the desk in the Bureau what I required, hoping she would advise me, when another, more elderly, woman came to her side and said:

" 'I think Mrs. D'Arcy Devilin would like to see this young woman.'

" 'She is not interested in Betty Sheffield?' the Secretary asked.

" 'No,' the elderly woman replied, 'she is not pretty enough.'

"I thought this sounded rather strange; but before I could ask any questions I was led into a small room which I guessed was where employers interviewed applicants for an engagement."

Selina drew a deep breath.

"Seated there was the smartest and most elegant lady I had ever seen."

Quintus Tiverton was listening intently and, as Selina continued her story, her voice low and hesitating, trembling sometimes over her words, he gained a very vivid picture of what had occurred.

He realised—as Selina had been unable to—the implications that lay behind the conversations, and how easily a girl from the country could have been bemused and bewildered by the sophistication of the woman who held out so tempting a situation.

Mrs. D'Arcy Devilin, with her full, rustling satin skirts, her elegant taffeta pelisse, and her bonnet trimmed with floating feathers, had looked to Selina like a being from another world.

She and her parents had lived very quietly in Little Cobham.

Although she occasionally had glimpses of the ladies of the County when they visited her mother or when she herself went to parties or Receptions at the Squire's or at the High Sheriff's Annual Assembly, Mrs. Devilin was more striking and certainly smarter than anyone she had ever seen before.

She was to learn later that it was Parisian chic, but at the moment she was concerned not only in admiring the fashionable figure who scrutinised her from head to foot, but in feeling slightly embarrassed by the sharpness of the lady's voice as she questioned her, and the penetrating glance of her dark eyes.

"I require a companion for my niece who lives with me in Paris," she said, "and I cannot bear to have ugly or gauche women round me. I want somebody who is educated, who understands how to be charming to the many important people who frequent my house, and who has at least a smattering of the graces that are essential for every young lady of fashion."

"I . . . I am . . . not certain . . . what those . . . a-are, Ma'am," Selina stammered.

"You will need to dance; you will need deportment; you will need to talk on many subjects, but, most of all, to be able to listen."

"I am sure I can do that," Selina said.

"You are certainly quite presentable," the lady went on in her hard voice. "At the same time, your clothes are lamentable."

"I understand, Madam, this young woman comes from the country," the woman from the Bureau interposed.

Mrs. Devilin gave her an impatient look.

"I think, Mrs. Hunt, I should prefer to interview this girl alone."

"Of course, Madam, I quite understand," Mrs. Hunt replied.

She bobbed a curtsey and went from the room, leaving Selina standing nervously in front of Mrs. Devilin.

"You may sit down," the latter said condescendingly. "And now answer my questions truthfully and accurately."

"I will try to do that," Selina replied in her soft voice.

"You are an orphan?"

"Yes, Ma'am."

"What relations have you?"

Selina wondered why it should matter that she had an Uncle with whom she could live until she found employment; a cousin in Scotland whom she never saw, and another in Cornwall who was so old that it was no use writing any further letters to her.

"You are quite prepared to come to France?" Mrs. Devilin asked.

"I should love to travel," Selina answered, "and I have always longed especially to see France and Italy."

"I live in Paris," Mrs. Devilin said. "Can you come with me tomorrow?"

"Yes, there is no reason why I should not," Selina answered.

"Your Uncle will not prevent you going?"

"No, indeed, Ma'am! He would be glad to think that I have employment, even though it is in another country."

"Very well, you can meet me at Sheriff's Hotel tomorrow morning at half after nine o'clock. Bring few clothes with you. I shall have to fit you out in Paris. You would be a laughing stock there in what you are wearing now."

Excited by the interview, Selina went back to her Uncle to tell him that she need no longer be an encumbrance to him.

"Paris?" he said reflectively. "From all I hear, Paris is not the city for a young girl alone."

"I do not expect Mrs. Devilin's niece would be allowed to go anywhere unchaperoned, Uncle Bartram," Selina had answered. "Mrs. Devilin appeared to me to be very strict."

"That is what I hope," her Uncle said. "You are

quite certain that you are wise to accept the first position you are offered? After all, there might be others more to your liking."

"This one is very much to my liking, Uncle Bartram," Selina replied. "You know how Papa always used to tell me about his travels abroad when he was in the Army. It is so wonderful to think that I can see a little of the world."

"I suppose it is all right," her Uncle said grudgingly. "Perhaps we should make some enquiries about this Mrs. Devilin. You say she was known to the Agency?"

"She was indeed. When she called Mrs. Hunt in and said she would engage me, Mrs. Hunt said:

" 'I only hope, Madam, that you have found the other young girls I have provided you with in the past to be satisfactory.'

"Mrs. Devilin laughed.

" 'Too satisfactory, Mrs. Hunt! They were so attractive and so charming that both of them have married. One to a very rich man, another to a nobleman!'

" 'That's nice for them, Madam,' Mrs. Hunt exclaimed.

" 'But a nuisance for me!' Mrs. Devilin replied. 'That is why I have come to visit you again; for I must say I am very satisfied with the service you have given me.'

" 'We do our best, Madam,' Mrs. Hunt replied. 'And may I say that we are by far the largest and the most exclusive Domestic Bureau in London. In fact our clientele is very distinguished. As I often remark to my assistant that it reads almost like a page from Debrett!' "

Selina, having related the story, waited for her Uncle's comment.

"It certainly sounds satisfactory, Selina," he had said.

At the same time, there was some doubt in his voice and Selina knew he was still perturbed at the thought of her going away to Paris. But for her it was an excitement beyond words.

She had been unable to sleep that night after she had packed her small leather trunk and had lain awake al-

ternately thanking God for looking after her and eagerly anticipating all that she might see in Paris.

She and Mrs. Devilin had travelled by train to Dover, crossed the Channel, and then taken a train for
Paris.

It had been a long and tiring journey, but they had
journeyed second-class in what seemed to Selina luxurious comfort.

It was only when she arrived in Paris that she had
been a little surprised to learn that Mrs. Devilin's niece
was not in the house.

It was a long, narrow, grey building in what she
learnt was the fashionable part of Paris, just off the
Rue de St. Honoré.

She had supposed that it belonged to Mrs. Devilin,
but from some remarks that were made by a servant
she learnt that it was only rented and that Mrs. Devilin
had not even seen it until her return from England.

It was Mrs. Devilin's husband, Mr. D'Arcy, who had
made all the arrangements. He was a middle-aged man,
flashily over-dressed, with bold eyes which made Selina
shrink away from him as soon as they met.

He looked her over slowly in a manner which she
felt was impertinent, almost as if she were a horse for
sale. Then he said:

"I congratulate you, Celestine. I could not have done
better myself!"

"I thought you would be pleased," Mrs. Devilin replied. "You have told him we are arriving?"

"He is all impatience, but he will have to wait a little
longer while you buy this child some clothes."

"I am well aware of that," Mrs. Devilin answered.
"Tell the dress-maker to come here first thing in the
morning and to bring with her everything she has. She
knows the type of thing we want."

"Yes, of course," D'Arcy Devilin replied.

Selina could not understand what they were talking
about.

She was shown to her room and a man-servant who
she thought had a familiar manner carried up her
trunk.

What puzzled her was that the house was so small.

She discovered that there was only one other bed-room on the same floor as her own, and that was occupied by Mrs. Devilin.

There was a small Sitting-Room on the ground floor, where she was given a meal before she went to bed, and she imagined that the first floor contained the Salon where doubtless they would sit the following day.

She was however too tired to worry her head particularly about the house, or indeed about herself. Instead she leant out of the window before she went to bed, trying to see in the darkness what Paris looked like.

The following morning the dress-maker arrived and Mrs. Devilin gave her orders in the sharp, authoritative tone which on the journey Selina had found rather disturbing, and indeed at times frightening.

She was very sensitive to atmosphere, and there was something about Mrs. Devilin which on further acquaintance made her feel like a cat who is having her fur rubbed the wrong way.

However, although Mrs. Devilin's tone was sharp, she had always spoken to Selina pleasantly.

"When shall I see your niece?" Selina asked as the dress-maker took her measurements.

"Later," Mrs. Devilin replied indifferently. "She is out of Paris at the moment."

"Then could I see a little of the city, if there is time?" Selina asked tentatively.

"There will be no time for that this afternoon," Mrs. Devilin replied. "After you have been fitted for your gowns, the hair-dresser is coming to wash your hair. After that we have several small items to buy, like shoes, gloves, a night-gown or two. Then I want you to rest before this evening."

"What is happening this evening?" Selina asked, her eyes sparkling.

She wondered if perhaps Mrs. Devilin was taking her to a theatre or if there was to be a party.

It was all very exciting and quite unlike anything she had expected in the way of work.

Mrs. Devilin did not reply at the time, but later in the afternoon she said to Selina:

"I have something to tell you; something which I know will please you very much."

"What is it?" Selina asked.

"There is a gentleman who is anxious to marry you."

"To marry me?" Selina exclaimed in utter astonishment.

"He is very rich and very distinguished," Mrs. Devilin answered, "and you are in fact an extremely fortunate young woman."

"But why should he want to marry me?" Selina asked. "He has never seen me."

"I have told him how beautiful you are, and as he is a widower he needs a wife."

"I cannot believe it is . . . true!" Selina said. "Who is this . . . gentleman?"

"He is the Marquis de Valpré," Mrs. Devilin answered, "a very old friend of mine. To be frank with you, Selina, he asked me if when I went to London I would try to find him a young and charming wife."

"B-but there must be . . . plenty of . . . women he knows in . . . France," Selina stammered.

"He is very partial to English girls, especially when they are fair-haired," Mrs. Devilin said with a smile. "Let me impress upon you again, Selina, that he is very important; in fact one of the most important members of French society. The Valprés are an ancient aristocratic family."

"I am of course very . . . honoured that he should . . . think of me," Selina said, "but you will understand, Ma'am, that I . . . could not . . . marry anyone I did not . . . love."

"My dear child, you are in France!" Mrs. Devilin said scornfully. "Marriages in France are always arranged. There is no question of love until after the couple have become man and wife."

"It is different in England," Selina said, "at least amongst ordinary people, although I believe the noble families do still have their marriages arran . . ."

Her voice died away because she saw an expression on Mrs. Devilin's face which frightened her.

"Are you going to be tiresome and difficult over this?" she asked.

There was something hard and inflexible in her voice which made Selina wince.

"No . . . indeed," Selina answered. "I would . . . like to meet the . . . M-Marquis and . . . talk to him. Perhaps when we . . . get to . . . know each other . . ."

"When you get to know him I am certain you will love him—if that is what you are looking for," Mrs. Devilin said contemptuously. "It should not be difficult when you remember that for a penniless and unimportant girl like yourself, it would be wonderful to have money and beautiful clothes and to move in the wealthy and glamourous social circles of Paris."

She gave a little smile.

"They say there has never been any period so extravagant or luxurious as the Second Empire; the jewels are magnificent, Selina; the clothes defy description. The Marquis can make you one of the most envied women in Paris."

It certainly sounded marvellous, Selina thought. At the same time, she had never imagined that anything like this would happen to her.

She had dreamt that there would be a man somewhere in the world who would love her and who would ask her to be his wife! But just to have a marriage arranged with a man she had never seen and of whom she knew nothing was frightening.

Mrs. Devilin swept any protests or arguments away from her lips.

"You will meet the Marquis tonight," she said. "You will dine with him alone, and you will find him charming, experienced, a man of the world, and if you play your cards cleverly, Selina—very generous."

Selina did not understand what she meant by that but she made up her mind that if she did not like the Marquis, she would refuse to marry him whatever Mrs. Devilin or anyone else might say.

At the same time, she realised that she had very little money of her own. In fact she was half afraid that there would not be enough to pay her fare back to England.

She had the feeling that if she did not do what Mrs. Devilin wanted there would be no question of her re-

taining her job, as she would be dispensed with ruth-
lessly and doubtless without compensation.

She did not wish to dwell on what might happen
then; she merely tried to tell herself optimistically that
if the Marquis was as charming as Mrs. Devilin had
said, she might like him and even in time come to love
him.

It was strange, Selina thought to herself, that she had
expected to find employment, and yet now she was to
be married.

Everyone had always said that marriage was the only
career open to a young woman, and apparently that
was the truth.

But marriage with an unknown man was something
she had never envisaged even in her moments of
deepest despair!

She had had plenty of such moments when she had
realised after her father's death, so unexpectedly from a
stroke, that he had left no money to provide for her future.

After her mother's death Selina had run the house
economically with one servant, and her father had always seemed to be satisfied with her efforts.

They had been poor, but somehow, one way or another, they had managed to be reasonably comfortable.

But to find herself completely penniless was something she had never anticipated, and she had lain in
bed shivering night after night at the thought of what
lay ahead, and how for the first time she must learn to
fend for herself.

But now, according to Mrs. Devilin, she was to
marry somebody very rich and charming; somebody
who would protect her and take care of her.

She would be a member of Parisian society and, although she had no idea what that entailed, she thought
it would be very unlike anything she had ever imagined
living quietly in Little Cobham.

She rested after she and Mrs. Devilin had been shopping. Selina had seen little of Paris and found the
sight of it exhilarating.

She had read about Baron Haussman and the building programme with which he and the Emperor Napoleon III had transformed the city.

"There is so much I want to explore," Selina had told herself when they had gone back to the house. "Perhaps I can persuade the Marquis to take me driving. He is certain to have fine horses and I want to see the place de la Concorde, the Champs Élysées, and the Bois."

She had lain down and rested as Mrs. Devilin had told her to do. When the maid came to call her she brought with her a gown which had just arrived from the dress-maker's.

Of white silk and lace, it made Selina look very young, but at the same time it had a chic and sophistication she had not anticipated.

The décolletage was very low—too low for modesty, she thought—the tight bodice revealing the soft curves of her breasts and the wide satin sash accentuating the smallness of her waist.

At the back the gown cascaded out with frill upon frill of white tulle which as she walked rippled behind her like tiny waves.

The crinoline had been discarded the previous year; the dresses were now swept backwards and the new fashionable silhouette appeared very strange in Selina's eyes.

At the same time she knew that she looked prettier than she ever had in her whole life. Her hair, which had been washed earlier in the day, was arranged by the *coiffeur* to fall in long ringlets at the back of her head.

Before she put on her gown, Mrs. Devilin came to her room to touch up her face with a hint of powder, to redden her lips with salve, and add a touch of mascara to her eye-lashes.

"I do not think my mother would have approved of my using cosmetics," Selina said shyly.

"In Paris you would look naked if you appeared without them," Mrs. Devilin replied sharply, "and I want you to look particularly alluring tonight. First impressions, as you well know, Selina, are important, and I wish the Marquis to think you beautiful."

Selina was nearly ready when to her surprise Mr. Devilin came to the door of her bed-room.

"Get her to sign this, Celestine," he said to his wife.

He handed Mrs. Devilin a paper. Then he said:

"I am leaving now. Tell the girl not to mention the fact that I have been here."

"I had not forgotten," Mrs. Devilin replied.

She took the paper and gestured to the maid to leave the room. Then she said to Selina:

"You heard what my husband said? It is important that you do not mention him to the Marquis."

"Why not?" Selina asked.

"Because the Marquis believes that I am a widow."

"A widow?" Selina exclaimed.

"It is a long story," Mrs. Devilin said quickly, "and I will not bore you with it, but I was married to Mr. Devilin. Then he left me for some time and I thought he was dead. I met the Marquis and told him I was a widow. Shortly afterwards Mr. Devilin reappeared."

She paused to add:

"I have not had an opportunity of explaining to the Marquis that he is back in my life. I am sure you will understand, Selina, and keep my secret."

"But of course," Selina said quickly.

"Now here is a little paper I want you to sign," Mrs. Devilin went on.

"What is it?" Selina asked.

"Oh, it is just something official to do with your being in Paris," Mrs. Devilin said lightly. "It is in French, so you will not understand it."

"I can read French," Selina answered. "Papa was very insistent that I should speak languages well, and as I always hoped that one day I would have the opportunity to travel, I not only had lessons in French and German, but I also read a lot of books in both languages."

She thought that Mrs. Devilin looked annoyed.

"Well, perhaps I had better explain," she said after a moment, "that if the Marquis gives you money, I shall expect, as I brought you to Paris at my expense, to have my share of it."

"I do not understand," Selina said.

"It is more difficult with jewellery," Mrs. Devilin went on. "Of course, you will give me a brooch or a bracelet from time to time, but money is easier. I will collect a certain sum—it depends what you receive—from you every week. I will not allow you to cheat me, Selina, or try to hide away what is my just reward for bringing the Marquis into your life."

"But surely," Selina asked in a bewildered voice, "you would not ask me to give away my husband's money without consulting him? And anyway, if he wishes you to have it, can he not give it to you himself?"

"You will sign this paper," Mrs. Devilin said in the voice which Selina feared, "or you will not meet the Marquis. And what is more, I shall turn you out onto the streets without a penny to your name, or a rag to your back."

There was something violent in the way she spoke and Selina said quickly:

"But of course I will sign the paper . . . it is just that . . . I do not want any . . . trouble with the . . . Marquis about it."

"There is no reason for him to know anything about our little arrangement," Mrs. Devilin said. "He has been generous to me in the past and doubtless will be again in the future. This is just a secret between you and me, Selina, but it is an obligation I shall expect you to keep."

"Yes . . . of course," Selina said nervously.

She looked at the document; one sentence seemed to jump out at her as she translated it: "Fifty percent as long as the association shall last."

"Can a marriage be described as an 'association'?" she asked herself.

Then Selina knew there was nothing she could do but sign, and hope that there would be no trouble about giving away money that might be given to her for other expenses.

Could Mrs. Devilin really mean to demand half the house-keeping money? Perhaps, if the stories were true, Frenchmen were so profligate with their wealth that the Marquis would never miss or question what she spent.

It was all rather bewildering, but she signed the paper and Mrs. Devilin, all smiles again, sprayed her with scent.

"The Marquis will be arriving at any moment," she said. "I have arranged for you to have dinner in the Salon. It is a very delicious and expensive meal, Selina, which has been brought from a Restaurant, the Maison d'Or, which fortunately is not far away. Be sure that he drinks plenty of wine and, above all, remember to make yourself charming. Do everything he asks of you."

"What might he ask me to do?" Selina asked a little nervously.

Mrs. Devilin's eyes narrowed.

"You will find out," she replied. "But remember, Selina, if you offend or upset the Marquis, I shall be angry—very angry indeed! In fact, I might turn you out of my house without a reference, and certainly without any wages."

With that Mrs. Devilin had gone from Selina's bedroom, leaving her alone.

She had however left the door open and soon afterwards Selina heard the front-door bell ring far below in the basement.

A servant answered it; then she heard a man's voice and knew that the Marquis was going up the first flight of stairs to the Salon.

Mrs. Devilin would be waiting there to greet him.

Selina suddenly felt very afraid.

What was happening to her? How could she have found herself in this strange situation where she was to marry a man she had never seen and if she did not please him was threatened with being thrown out into the streets?

How wise her Uncle had been in suggesting that they should have learnt something more about Mrs. Devilin before she went to France with her.

Selina's hands were cold and she was trembling when finally the man-servant knocked on her bed-room door and told her she was wanted downstairs in the Salon.

Feeling as if she was about to mount the guillotine,

Selina walked slowly down the stairs, the train of her white dress making a soft, silky sound as she moved.

She caught a glimpse of herself in the long mirror and realised that she looked beautiful, and yet very unlike her real self.

Her eyes were wide and dark and she felt as if it were impossible to breathe.

The servant opened the door of the Salon.

"Mademoiselle Selina Wade, Monsieur le Marquis!" he announced.

Selina advanced into the room a few paces and then stood rooted to the spot, unable to move.

Chapter Two

Selina's voice died away and then she said with a little trembling gesture of her hands:

"I cannot ... describe to you what he ... looked like."

Quintus Tiverton with his eyes on her face said quietly:

"I think it important, Selina, for you to tell me every detail. I have heard of the Marquis de Valpré, but I have never actually met him."

"He was ... old," Selina said after a moment, "much older than I had expected, and small ... hardly as tall as I am. ... But it was not ... that. ..."

"What was it?" Quintus Tiverton asked.

"It was the expression on his face. He looked ... well, I suppose the right word is ... debauched ... and repulsive and quite unlike any other ... man I had ever seen in my life."

She went on hesitatingly to describe how for several seconds she had been unable to move and the Marquis had come across the Salon to take her cold fingers in his and raise them to his lips.

"You are entrancing!" he said, "and far more beautiful than I expected."

"You ... you are really the ... Marquis de Valpré?" Selina asked.

She had a wild idea at the back of her mind that this was a joke; that the real Marquis was someone quite different, and that this small old man was impersonating him.

"That is my name," the Marquis replied. "But come and sit down, Selina. I am sure you would like a glass of wine."

Selina took the glass he gave her into her hand sim-

24

ply because she felt she had not the strength to refuse it.

She kept looking at the Marquis as if she felt he must be a figure from a nightmare and not the man that Mrs. Devilin had told her she was to marry.

He was smartly dressed, in fact he was more elegantly attired than any man she had ever seen.

But the way he looked at her under hooded eye-lids with a smile on his pale lips made every instinct in her body tell her that he was dangerous.

She wondered wildly what she should do! Should she run away at once, after telling the Marquis, before he could say any more, that she would not marry him and could never contemplate doing so?

Then before she could make up her mind the door opened and servants appeared, bringing in their dinner.

The Marquis put out his hand to take Selina's and help her from the sofa on which she was sitting towards the table that was set in the centre of the room.

At the touch of his fingers she knew that her instinctive first reaction had been right; for now she felt a revulsion such as she had never known, and her whole body shrank from him.

"Let us eat, pretty lady, and you must tell me about your fascinating little self," the Marquis said.

A flunkey wearing an elaborate livery, who Selina thought must be the Marquis's own servant, held a chair first for her and then for his Master.

For the first time Selina looked round her and realised that the Salon was larger than she had expected.

There were elaborate pelmets over the curtained windows and Louis XIV console tables against the paneled walls with mirrors above them.

The whole room was decorated in pale blue and grey and lit only by candles. It had a charm which was singularly lacking in the other rooms in the house.

Then Selina noticed that at the far end of the room there was a door which was half-open. Through it, to her surprise, she could see a bed.

That room too was lit by candles, and she could see them alight in candelabra on either side of the draped and canopied bed.

'That must be,' she thought to herself, 'where Mrs. Devilin's niece will sleep when she arrives.'

Then like a streak of lightning she realised that there was no niece.

The whole story had been just a fabrication! Had not Mrs. Devilin said that the Marquis had asked her before she went to England to find him a wife?

But if there was no niece, then why were the candles lit in the adjoining room?

As the questions rushed through her mind Selina realised that the Marquis was talking.

"There are so many things in Paris that I want to show you," he said, "Because I understand that you have never been here before."

"N-no," Selina faltered.

It was the first word she had spoken since she came into the room and she thought how gauche her shyness and her fear must make her appear.

But there was a look in the Marquis's eyes that she could only interpret as admiration; and there was also something else, something to which she dared not put a name.

"This is a city of beautiful women," the Marquis ccontinued, "and I know, Selina—and I am never mistaken in my judgment—that you will eclipse them all."

"I am afraid you are ... mistaken ... *Monsieur*," Selina answered.

She thought to herself that if she was wise she would make it clear to the Marquis right away that, whatever he had to suggest, it was of no interest and that never, whatever inducements he might offer, would she become his wife.

'There is something horrible and disgusting about him!' she told herself, then wondered how she could be so sure.

"Tomorrow," the Marquis said, as if she had not spoken, "I will take you driving in the Bois, and you shall see all the famous beauties parading in their carriages."

"Thank you," Selina said. "but I—I may have ... other things to do."

The Marquis shot her a sharp glance before he said:

"If you mean we should first visit a jeweller's, then I will not disappoint you. I wonder what stones will become you best. All women like diamonds, but they are almost too cold and hard for your young skin."

"I ... I did not ... mean that, *Monsieur*," Selina said quickly.

"Then what did you mean?" the Marquis enquired.

Selina looked uncomfortably at the servants waiting behind their chairs and with a smile on his lips the Marquis said:

"We will talk of such matters later on. Let me now tell you where else we will go. I shall wish to show you to my friends—to the audience at the Opera, who look more at the spectators than at the performers, and of course we must dine in La Grande Seize at the Café Anglais."

"Where is that?"

"That is where you will see all the millionaires with their beautiful ladies. Once again, may I say how proud I shall be to escort anyone so delectable."

There was no doubt, Selina told herself, that he was trying to be charming and endeavouring to entertain her.

She knew that it was wrong to find fault, but it was hard to listen to what he was saying when she could feel his eyes watching her.

She was acutely embarrassed by the low-cut décolletage of her dress and, when the Marquis was helping himself to one of the delicious dishes that succeeded one another in a seemingly endless series, she gave her dress a little tug.

She endeavoured to pull it higher so that his eyes could not linger on the little valley between her breasts.

'After dinner I must tell him that I cannot marry him,' she planned, 'and if possible I must tell him before he proposes. He will feel humiliated that he should be refused by an unknown and unimportant English girl! Nevertheless, I must make him understand and beg him not to make Mrs. Devilin angry with me.'

Even to think of Mrs. Devilin made Selina tremble.

There had been so much violence in her voice when she had said that if she did not do what the Marquis wanted she would turn her out of the house without a reference and without any money.

'In which case,' Selina asked herself, 'how can I get back to England?'

Perhaps the Marquis would be understanding. After all, she told herself, he would not wish to marry a bride who was reluctant and who did not like him.

She drew in her breath.

"Like" was too pleasant a word. She did not know why, but she actually hated the Marquis. It might seem unreasonable, but the emotion was there; she hated him. She knew that if he came near her she would want to scream.

Their dinner took a long time and while the Marquis talked Selina tried frantically to plan what she would say to him once the servants had left the room.

Finally they withdrew, the last to leave being the Marquis's own man, who looked round him and then, quite unnecessarily, Selina thought, snuffed out some of the candles.

The Marquis walked towards the fireplace and as the door closed behind the flunkey he said:

"At last we are alone. How delightful this is, Selina, and how entrancing you are in every way. It will be an excitement such as I have not experienced for a long time to teach you the joys of love."

Desperately Selina knotted her fingers together and said in a very small voice:

"I am afraid ... *Monsieur* ... there has been some ... misunderstanding."

"What sort of misunderstanding?" the Marquis asked.

He held a glass of cognac in his hand, and as he sipped it Selina replied:

"Mrs. Devilin told me I must ... do as you want ... but it would be ... impossible."

"Nothing is impossible!" The Marquis said, "not where you and I are concerned, Selina, and I find you very desirable. In fact you have captivated me completely!"

He put out his arms towards her as he spoke, but Se-

lina sprang from the sofa before he could touch her to
stand looking at him with frightened eyes.

"I am sorry, *Monsieur* . . . but I must make it very
clear now and at once . . . that I cannot—"

She got no further because the Marquis had risen to
his feet and had moved towards her with his arms out-
stretched, and only with a struggle was Selina free of
him.

She felt her gown tear as she ran away to the other
side of the table to stand with her breath coming
quickly, looking at the Marquis as he moved also into
the centre of the room.

"You are adorable!" he said and his voice was thick.
"You are like a little bird who will flutter helplessly but
cannot avoid being captured."

"You must . . . listen to me!" Selina cried desperately.

"We will talk later," the Marquis answered. "For
the moment I want to kiss the softness of your lips and
feel your body close to mine."

There was something in the way he said the last
words which made Selina draw in her breath with
shock.

The fact that the Marquis's servant had extinguished
some of the lights in the Salon made those in the bed-
room appear to gleam more brightly.

Now she was acutely conscious of the lighted room
and the candle-lit bed.

Why was it there and for whom was it waiting?

As if the Marquis read her thoughts he said silkily:

"You are to be mine, Selina. You need not question
my generosity, but I want you and you cannot escape
me."

"You cannot . . . come near . . . me!" Selina replied.
"I will not . . . let you!"

"And how will you stop me?" he asked.

Now he came round the table towards her.

With a little cry she ran towards the door but before
she could reach it the Marquis moved with a swiftness
she had not expected from him and was there before
her.

Once again he put out his arms and drew her almost roughly towards him.

With a strength she had not known she possessed, Selina fought herself free to stand with her back to a serving table, facing the Marquis.

"Let me go!" she whispered. "Please . . . let me go."

Even as she spoke she realised that such a plea was hopeless.

There was a fire in his eyes that she had before never seen in any man's, and there was an expression on his face which made him look almost like a demon.

He stood looking at the tumultuous rise and fall of her breasts, at the paleness of her cheeks, and the terror in her large eyes! Innocent though she was, Selina knew that she excited him.

Slowly and deliberately he took off his close-fitting evening-coat and threw it on the nearest chair.

His shirt was of the very finest linen, so transparent that she could see the thick, dark mat of hairs on his chest. They revolted her even as everything else about him was repulsive.

"I shall catch you in the end, Selina," he said, "and let me tell you, I enjoy a chase. A woman who is complacent can be a bore, but someone as young and desirable as you can be even more alluring when she is hard to get!"

He took a step towards her as he spoke, and now at last Selina understood what he intended to do.

It was not marriage the Marquis was offering her, but something so humiliating and degrading that she knew she would rather die than endure it.

He was coming nearer and, while once again she wanted to run away from him, she felt as if her legs had suddenly become too weak to carry her.

She put her hands behind her as if to hold on to the table for support, and as she did so realised that the cutlery that had not been used during their dinner was still arranged on the sideboard.

Almost without her conscious volition, her fingers tightened over a wooden handle as the Marquis, his eyes on hers until she felt as if he hypnotised her, reached her.

"You thrill me," he said, "as no woman has made me thrill for a long time. It fascinates me to realise that you are afraid of me. It is because I am a man, Selina, a man who will turn you from a frightened child into a woman."

He spoke in a slow, silky voice, as if the very sound of his own words excited him, and now once again he reached out his arms.

"I want you!" the Marquis cried. "You are mine, Selina, and there is no escape!"

His arms went round her and, as they did so, Selina raised her hand which clutched the wooden handle and struck with all her strength.

She saw in the candle-light the gleam of the thin, pointed blade, and felt it force its way into the Marquis's chest with an almost surprising ease.

He gave a groan, his eyes widened, and his mouth fell open. Then as both hands went up towards the hilt of the knife protruding from his chest, he staggered backwards and fell.

His body made surprisingly little noise as he crashed onto the carpet. While Selina stood, her left hand still holding on to the serving-table, staring at him, the blood flowed crimson over the whiteness of his shirt.

For a moment she could not believe that it had really happened; that she had prevented the Marquis from taking her in his arms and in doing so had killed him.

She was sure that he was dead because after the first groan that had come from his lips as she struck at him, he had made no sound. His mouth had opened further and his eyes had widened, but now there was no expression in them.

His whole body seemed to have shrunk and as he lay there his face appeared to be even more debauched and repulsive.

For a long time Selina could not move. Only the blood, red and horrifying, seemed to spread over the Marquis's chest.

Then suddenly with a sound which should have been a scream but which was stuck in her throat, she ran to the door.

"Help! Help!" she called.

It was difficult to explain to Quintus Tiverton what had happened after that, but she thought that perhaps she had lost consciousness.

When finally she could hear what was going on, she found herself being cursed and abused by Mrs. Devilin, but she was incapable of understanding what the woman was saying to her.

She lay with her eyes closed and hoped Mrs. Devilin would think that she was still insensible.

It was only after a long delay that Selina realised that a servant had been sent to fetch Mr. Devilin and that he had come into the Salon to stand looking down at the Marquis's dead body.

"Who knows of this?" he asked sharply in French.

"No-one," Mrs. Devilin replied. "His servant left after dinner and when I sent Jacques for you I did not say why I needed you."

Mr. Devilin had shut the door to the Salon when he entered it; now he crossed the room to Selina's side.

"You little fool!" he said angrily. "Why the devil did you want to kill him?"

"Hand her over to the police," Mrs. Devilin cried hysterically. "Let her be punished for the crime she has committed! The guillotine is waiting for her!"

"Are you insane?" Mr. Devilin asked angrily. "Do you suppose that if the police question her she will not betray you, and I might be involved? There is too much at stake, Celestine, to take risks of that sort."

"Then what can we do?" Mrs. Devilin enquired.

"You and this girl must get out of the country," he answered. "Take her to Baden-Baden and get her off your hands to the first idiot who offers for her."

He paused for a moment and then he said:

"It is entirely your fault for not breaking her in before she met the Marquis."

"She seemed so pliable, so simple," Mrs. Devilin said defensively.

"Well, she has proved she is not," he retorted. "It should not be beyond your powers to persuade her one way or another to do as she is told."

He glanced again towards the dead body on the ground before he said:

"I have expended quite a lot of money on her—I want that back as well as what the Marquis paid you."

"He did pay, thank goodness," Mrs. Devilin said in a low voice. "You will find it downstairs locked in a drawer."

"I will take it and clear away everything else as soon as you have gone."

"You mean us to go—now?"

"Of course," he replied. "I will order a carriage to take you to the Station, where you can wait for a train. There is sure to be one at about seven o'clock in the morning."

He paused again before he said:

"Change your name, of course, and hers too. Drum it into the chit's head that she has never heard of a 'Mrs. Devilin' or of me."

"She thinks you are my husband."

"As far as she is concerned, I don't exist. Surely you can beat that into her?"

"I will beat a good many things into her before I am finished," Mrs. Devilin said viciously.

"It's a pity you didn't do so before this happened. The Marquis was a good source of income, as you well know."

"How will you explain in the morning that he is dead?" Mrs. Devilin asked.

"I know nothing about it," Mr. Devilin replied. "It is you they will be looking for, Celestine."

"So that's your game!"

"Why not? As far as I am concerned I have never heard of him. It will be hard, Celestine—make no mistake—to connect me with him in any way, and if you know what's good for you, you will not attempt to do so, even if the police catch up with you."

"I shall see that I keep clear of them," Mrs. Devilin answered, "even if I have to kill this crazy creature in the meantime."

"Another dead body would be an embarrassment," Mr. Devilin replied. "Just make certain that she is too frightened to talk. It should not be difficult."

He turned as he spoke and, taking Selina by the arm as she lay back in the chair into which she had collapsed when she felt faint, dragged her roughly to her feet.

"In the future you will do as you are told," he said, "or you will end up in the Seine, as dead as the man you have murdered. You are lucky that we are prepared to save your skin and your pretty head. But make no mistake—if you try to betray us I will kill you!"

He spoke ferociously, with his face close to Selina's and then as instinctively she stepped backwards he slapped her hard across the face.

"Go and put together what clothes you have into a trunk," he ordered. "You will be dealt with later, make no mistake about it."

"I can promise you that!" Mrs. Devilin said.

Selina, with her hand to her burning cheek, walked a little unsteadily towards the door, averting her eyes from the Marquis's body, lying on the floor, and went upstairs to her own bed-room.

Only then did she wonder despairingly how she could ever escape from this nightmare of horror which seemed to be holding her tighter and tighter in its grip.

"God . . . help . . . me," she whispered.

As Selina finished speaking she swept back some of her fair hair from her forehead with fingers that trembled.

"We caught a train very early in the morning," she went on, "and we should have reached Baden-Baden tonight if there had not been the fall of rock on the line. There were other people in our carriage and Mrs. Devilin did not speak to me."

She stopped and then said:

"I should not have said that. Her name is now Madame Bryen and I am her niece."

"So this is the first time she has beaten you?" Quintus Tiverton asked.

"Yes, but she will do it . . . again, and because I am so . . . frightened . . . in the . . . end I will . . . have to do what she . . . wants me to."

"You know what that is?" he asked.

"Mrs. Dev—I mean, Madame Bryen—told me . . . tonight when she came up . . . here after I had gone to bed. . . . She admitted that the Marquis had never . . . thought of marrying me . . . he wanted me . . . to be his . . . mistress."

Quintus Tiverton saw the colour come into Selina's cheeks at the word. It made her even more beautiful, he thought, than she was already.

"I was so . . . foolish that I did not . . . understand," Selina murmured.

Quintus Tiverton understood a great deal more from the story than she had told him.

He remembered hearing that the Marquis de Valpré had a penchant for very young girls, and even in the dissolute, lascivious Paris of the Second Empire he was reputedly a debauchée.

He also had a vague suspicion of who the man was that Selina had innocently thought of as Mrs. Devilin's husband.

There were two or three procurers in Paris who supplied the nobility and even the Emperor with women. They amassed enormous fortunes, and because it was possible, if they wished to do so, to blackmail their distinguished clients, they had tremendous power.

English girls, young and fair-haired, were continually imported to Paris and there was little the authorities could do about it in either country.

The patrons who seduced them were in a position to stifle any official enquiries, and after all it was almost universally accepted that women were only there to be the playthings of men.

The Second Empire was the golden age of the courtesan, and *les grandes cocottes* had made Paris a by-word for vice and debauchery which was unsurpassed in any other capital in Europe.

Quintus Tiverton was well aware that a girl who was not as sensitive or well bred as Selina might have adapted herself, once she had been introduced to a world where her beauty would have attracted men of importance and intelligence.

Like the other *demi-mondaines*, she could have

amassed an enormous fortune and lived in luxury that
was beyond the dreams of ordinary women.

But he could understand that Selina could not toler-
ate a man like the Marquis de Valpré. She had known,
without being told and while being entirely ignorant of
the world in which he lived, that he was wicked and
that any contact with him would harm her.

Quintus Tiverton wondered now how it would be
possible to save her from the predicament in which she
found herself. Then coldly and logically his brain told
him that it was impossible.

He had his own problems and there was no point in
trying to saddle himself with hers.

He looked at her facing him, and the light from the
candles told him that her beauty would involve her in a
thousand impossible situations from which only a husband could protect her.

Deliberately he looked away from the appeal in her
eyes to say:

"I am very sorry for you, Selina. I only wish I could
help."

"P-please . . . help me," she said in a voice he could
hardly hear.

"The only thing I can do," he went on, "is to give
you some money. Hide it somewhere safely, and if you
can escape from this woman when you reach Baden-
Baden, you should take the train to Holland. There you
can book a passage on a ship to England."

He felt in his pockets as he spoke and said with a
smile:

"I am afraid I am also somewhat pressed at the moment, so I cannot give you as much as I should like to
do. But here is ten pounds, which will cover your fares.
Be careful that your jailor does not find it."

He put the notes down on the bed in front of
Selina, but she did not touch them.

"How can I get . . . away?" she asked. "Perhaps she
will have . . . another man like the . . . Marquis waiting
for me at . . . Baden-Baden."

Quintus Tiverton was quite certain that Mrs. Devilin, or whatever she called herself, would have no diffi-

culty in finding a man to bargain for Selina once he had seen her.

Baden-Baden at this time of the year was filled with all the pimps and procurers from every capital of Europe.

If Mrs. Devilin required assistance in disposing of Selina, they would be only too happy to oblige.

The town would be full of millionaires who wanted to gamble in the Casino and be seen with beautiful women. Just as they wished to ride or drive superb horse-flesh. A mistress was a symbol of social and financial status.

The more money they spent on *cocottes*, the more they were admired by their contemporaries, and the more the women vied amongst themselves to incite envy by their possessions.

Quintus Tiverton could remember the outrageous extravagances that the courtesans of Paris inspired in their lovers.

Cora Pearl, an English *demi-mondaine* who was kept by the Duc de Morny, had a box of marrons glacés presented to her by one of her lovers, each separately wrapped in a thousand-franc note.

Prince Napoleon had offered her a large vanload of the most expensive orchids. She gave a supper-party, strewed the orchids over the floor, and, dressed as a sailor, danced the hornpipe on them.

Cora spent a fortune in entertaining. One day she wagered her guests that she would give them meat which none of them would dare cut.

She had herself served up on a huge silver salver, borne by four men. She was naked, with a sprinkling of parsley.

Quintus Tiverton could not imagine Selina doing such things at the moment. But perhaps the day would come.

It was a pity—a terrible pity—that anyone so lovely must suffer because of her beauty, but that after all was the way of the world!

"P-please," Selina pleaded, "please hide me. Please take me with you wherever you are going."

There was a child-like appeal in her voice which

Quintus Tiverton found hard to refuse. However, he hardened his heart.

"I am sorry," he replied, "but you do not know what you are asking. I am not a rich man, Selina."

"I do not want your money," she said. "If you can just . . . protect me until I can return to England . . . or perhaps find myself . . . respectable employment."

Quintus Tiverton could not help wondering what respectable work lay open to a girl as lovely as Selina. No woman with eyes in her head would be likely to employ her, and it seemed as if inevitably she would become a *cocotte* simply because she was too beautiful to be anything else.

"I would not be much of an . . . expense," Selina said, "and if I was with . . . you, I would not . . . feel . . . afraid."

"How do you know that?" Quintus Tiverton asked almost roughly. "You have never seen me before tonight. I may be as bad, or worse, than the Marquis de Valpré."

"I know you are kind," Selina said, "and . . . and a . . . gentleman."

"That is no reason for trusting me," Quintus Tiverton said defensively.

"But I know I can trust you," Selina persisted. "I know it inside me . . . just as I knew I could not . . . trust . . ."

She stopped as if she could not bear to make herself speak the words.

"I have told you that all I can do is to give you money," Quintus Tiverton said. "Wait until this woman, who has you in her clutches, goes out and leaves you alone, then escape."

As he spoke he knew that Mrs. Devilin would not be so stupid as to leave Selina alone unless she was locked in.

He had heard how in the brothels of London and Paris the women were virtual prisoners, and that once they were under the jurisdiction of a "madam" there was no possible escape.

After what had happened already, Mrs. Devilin would take no chances.

He looked at Selina and looked away again. The girl was so absurdly young.

As she had used her hands to illustrate what she was saying, she had forgotten to hold up the sheet and through the plain cotton night-gown Quintus Tiverton could see the outline of her small breasts not yet fully matured.

Savagely he told himself that it was a disgrace to civilisation that women should be exploited in such a manner.

But how could he do anything about it?

Deliberately he rose to his feet.

"I am going to leave you to go to sleep, Selina," he said. "Hide the money I have given you, and perhaps when you reach Baden-Baden things will not be as bad as you anticipate."

Selina looked at him and he saw the terror in her eyes.

"She will . . . beat me . . . until I . . . do what she . . . wants me to do!"

"Damnit!" Quintus Tiverton said angrily, "there must be some way you can be free of her!"

Selina did not reply. She only looked at him, and he knew what she was thinking.

"It is impossible!" he said after a moment. "How can I arrive in Baden-Baden with empty pockets and a girl I have never seen until this evening? The whole thing is ridiculous!"

He walked across the room to stand staring down at the grate.

"You have picked the wrong man to help you, Selina," he said. "Do you know what I am?"

"Someone who has been very kind to me."

Quintus Tiverton turned round.

"I do not mean that," he said. "What you should know is that I am a gambler, and a gambler's livelihood is extremely precarious."

"I would be no . . . trouble . . . please take . . . me with you."

"It is an entreaty you should not make to me," he answered. "If I had any sense I would have left you crying, instead of coming in here and being made so sorry for you that I feel . . ."

He stopped speaking and walked a few steps across the room and back again.

"It is insane! You know that as well as I do."

"Could you . . . listen to . . . me?" Selina begged.

"Only if you have something sensible to say," he retorted.

"I think it is . . . sensible."

"Well—what is it?"

With a little gesture of her hand Selina indicated the place at the foot of the bed where he had sat before, and almost reluctantly he seated himself.

"I have just thought," Selina said in a breathless little voice, "that if you take me with you . . . to Baden-Baden or wherever you are . . . going, it might be possible for you to find me a husband—a real husband who would be . . . kind and . . . understanding."

Quintus Tiverton looked at her.

"You are prepared to accept marriage?" he asked.

Selina threw out her hands helplessly.

"What else can I do?" she asked. "I have no talents, I am not clever except at running a house. There must be a man somewhere who would not . . . frighten me, and I would make him a . . . good wife."

Quintus Tiverton did not answer for a moment and then he said:

"I suppose it is a possibility. I am sure, Selina, without flattering you, that there will be men, if we can find them, who will find your beauty so irresistible they will be prepared to produce a wedding-ring."

"Then please . . . may I come with . . . you?"

He looked at her for a long moment.

There was something ethereal, almost spiritual about her beauty which made him wonder if in fact he was dreaming and this whole conversation was a part of his imagination. Then he said almost harshly:

"If I take you with me will you promise to obey me? And if I find you a husband who, as you say, is decent and kind, will you accept him?"

He saw a sudden light in Selina's eyes and her face seemed to come alive with a new beauty.

"You mean . . . you will take me?"

"Only if you give me your word of honour that you will do as you are told."

"I . . . promise you . . . I give you my . . . word," Selina said, "if only you will take me . . . away from here."

"I believe in the morning I shall tell myself I am deranged and should see a Physician," Quintus Tiverton said, "but at the moment I feel there is no alternative."

"Can we go . . . now?" Selina asked.

"I want some sleep and so do you," Quintus Tiverton replied, "but we will leave the Inn before the other people are awake. At what time will Mrs. Devilin rise?"

"We were told tonight," Selina answered, "that we were to be downstairs at eight-thirty in the morning to wait for a conveyance to take us to the train."

"Very well," Quintus Tiverton said, "we will leave at six o'clock. I will knock on the wall at five-thirty. When you are dressed I will take you downstairs."

He looked round the room and saw Selina's square trunk standing beneath a window.

"We will be riding, so all you can bring with you is what you can roll up in a shawl or a cloak, to be fastened to the saddle."

He sighed and added:

"I suppose I shall have to contrive to buy you some gowns when we reach Baden-Baden."

"I . . . I am sure I can manage with what I have," Selina said.

Quintus Tiverton smiled.

"Unless I am mistaken, they are not the sort of garments to attract attention amongst a congregation of the best-dressed women in Europe."

"Must we go to Baden-Baden?" Selina asked nervously.

"That is my destination," Quintus Tiverton replied. "As I have told you, Selina, I am a gambler, and, I may add, without sounding conceited, a good one. To live by one's wits one has to be."

"You look so rich," Selina said, glancing at his elegantly cut coat and immaculate cravat.

"All part of the stock-in-trade," he said lightly. "You will learn, Selina, that we all have our stage props, and yours must be a collection of beautiful gowns."

"I cannot allow you to spend a lot of your money on me," Selina protested. "But perhaps when I am married I shall be able to pay you back."

"And of course, just like Mrs. Devilin, that is what I shall expect you to do," Quintus Tiverton said. "After all, if we are going to set out on this mad adventure, we might as well be successful in our adventuring. Pirates, like crooks, expect to carry off the spoils and the booty."

"It sounds exciting . . . and I am sure it . . . will be if I am with . . . you."

There was a little lilt in Selina's voice that had not been there before and Quintus Tiverton told himself that her eyes were shining like stars. Then he mocked himself for being sentimental.

"We are in business together, Selina," he said firmly, "and we must be business-like in everything we do."

"Yes, of course," she said in a tone which told him that she did not understand what he was trying to say.

"Never mind," he said as if to himself. "First we have to be careful that you are not apprehended before we leave the Inn if you are to escape from the clutches of the dragon who brought you here."

"That is what she is," Selina said, "a dragon—and a very frightening one! And you, of course, because you are rescuing me and are English, must be St. George!"

"Let me make it clear from the very beginning," Quintus Tiverton said firmly. "I am not a Saint, Selina, I am a hard-headed, hard-hearted gambler, and I have an unpleasant conviction that I have just staked a lot of money on what is likely to be an unlucky wager."

"No, you are wrong," Selina argued. "I am sure, quite sure, that I shall bring you luck! I do not know how or why, but I have the feeling inside me, and when I feel like this I am never wrong."

Quintus Tiverton picked up the notes he had put on the bed and rose to his feet.

"Let us hope you are right, Selina. At any rate, now go to sleep. We have a long way to go tomorrow and with the punishment you have received tonight you are likely to find riding extremely uncomfortable, to say the least of it."

"I do not mind," Selina said. "I do not mind anything as long as you will really take me with you."

She paused for a moment and he saw a sudden anxiety in her face as she added:

"You will ... take me? You will not ... disappear in the night so that in the morning I will find you ... gone?"

She looked at him pleadingly and he tried to resist the sensitiveness of her eyes and the wistfulness of her whole appearance, which seemed somehow to strike at his heart.

Just for a moment he considered telling her that he had changed his mind; that he could not involve himself in a situation that was likely to bring him so many difficulties and problems.

Quintus Tiverton had known a great many women in his life. As he travelled and spent some years in Paris, there had always been women reaching out their arms towards him, offering him their lips and the softness of their bodies.

He would have been a liar if he had not admitted that he knew a great deal more about the sex than most men of his age. And because of it he was certain that Selina was all she appeared to be.

She was innocent, pure, and good as few women he had met were good.

"In which case," he asked himself, "why in God's name am I saddling myself with her?"

A mistress was one thing. He had travelled with one often enough and found in most cases it was a mistake, for women were at their best when they were not transplanted from one country to another.

To find himself playing *duenna* to a girl who had hardly left the school-room, who knew nothing of life and certainly nothing of the type of society they would encounter at Baden-Baden, was an experience he had never had.

He could foresee all sorts of problems, all sorts of fantastic situations arising!

It suddenly struck him that if he really intended to try to find a husband for Selina, it would not be a propitious start for a prospective husband to suppose that she was his mistress.

"I tell you what we must do, Selina," he said aloud, "we must introduce ourselves as brother and sister."

She looked at him for a moment in surprise, and then she said:

"But of course! I was just thinking that perhaps people would think it a little strange for us to be traveling together without a chaperon."

"We can hardly take Mrs. Devilin along to play the part," Quintus Tiverton said laughingly.

Then he saw Selina shiver.

"Forget about her," he added sharply. "From this moment she has ceased to be of any importance in your life."

"Supposing . . . just supposing she . . . sees us in Baden-Baden? She could tell people that you are not my brother."

"I think that is unlikely," Quintus Tiverton said, "and once you are really free of her, Selina, she will give up the chase where you are concerned. After all, if she tried to expose you, she is well aware that you can expose her."

"Yes . . . of course," Selina agreed nervously.

"So from this moment on, you are my sister," Quintus Tiverton said. "Your name is Selina Tiverton, and as we journey tomorrow I will tell you a little about my family, just in case we encounter any of my friends in Baden-Baden."

"Will they not think it strange that you should suddenly produce a sister?"

"As it happens, I have one," he answered. "She is slightly younger than you and so has not yet appeared in society. But do not anticipate any more difficulties than there are likely to be already. Let us just accept things as they come."

He smiled and went on:

"That is actually my philosophy—to accept what the

fates bring me, even if it happens to be a young woman in trouble."

"How can I . . . thank you?" Selina asked.

"There is no need for you to do anything of the sort," he answered. "In fact, if there is one thing I dislike, it is people being obsequiously grateful. It always makes me feel uncomfortable."

"I should hate to do that," Selina said, "but you know I am deeply . . . overwhelmingly . . . grateful."

"Wait until we are free of this Inn and all it contains," Quintus Tiverton replied. "I am tired, Selina, and you have given me a lot to think about. I am going to bed, I hope to sleep. I suggest you do the same."

"You will not forget to wake me?" Selina said. "Suppose you oversleep?"

"I can always awake at any time I wish," Quintus Tiverton replied. "It is a trick I have taught myself over the years and it is exceedingly convenient. At exactly five-thirty you will hear me knock on the wall. Now I am going to lock you in, not to keep you from running away but to prevent any other visitors from disturbing your night's rest."

"I will try to sleep," Selina said, "although I wish tomorrow were . . . already here."

"It will come," he promised, "that is one thing of which we can be quite sure. Good-night, Selina, I hope I shall prove an adequate and commendable brother."

"I am very proud and grateful to be your sister," Selina said in a low voice.

He turned towards the door, and as he reached it he looked back.

The candle-light shimmering on the gold of Selina's hair and on her heart-shaped face showed her to be very different now from the terrified, weeping girl he had found when he first entered the room.

"Good-night," she said softly, "and . . . God bless you for being . . . so very . . . very kind."

Quintus Tiverton, locking the door from the outside, removed the key and went to his own attic.

As he did so he found himself remember that the last woman to say "God bless you" to him in that soft and gentle way had been his mother.

Chapter Three

It was very hot, the sky was cloudless, and now that Selina and Quintus Tiverton were away from the mountains it seemed impossible to believe that it had been so cold and windy the night before.

As they rode slowly down into the Oos valley they began to find the tall pines of the Black Forest surrounding them.

Selina was, as Quintus Tiverton had predicted, feeling very stiff and her back was extremely painful from the beating given her by Mrs. Devilin.

Nevertheless, she would have endured far worse pain without complaint because she was so ecstatically happy in the knowledge that she had escaped and no longer had to be afraid of what lay ahead.

When Quintus Tiverton had knocked on her wall she was already awake. She found it almost impossible to sleep for more than an hour or so because she was so apprehensive in case he left without her.

At his knock she jumped out of bed and began to dress quickly. Fortunately she had in her trunk a riding-habit she had worn at home in the summer.

Although it was made of an inexpensive material and Selina was certain that she would seem dowdy in it compared with the riders in Baden-Baden, the colour was extremely becoming.

The deep blue echoed the blue of her eyes, and she knew when she looked into the small, cracked mirror attached to the wall that the misery and fear which had seemed to disfigure her face yesterday had gone.

As Quintus Tiverton had commanded her to do, she packed all that she thought absolutely necessary into the cloak in which she had travelled from England.

She hesitated over the white gown which Mrs. Dev-

46

ilin had given her and which she had worn for her dinner with the Marquis.

Her first impulse was to turn from it in disgust and hope that she would never see it again because it would remind her all too forcibly of what had occurred.

Then with practical common sense she told herself that the gown was in fact extremely attractive and must have been very expensive. If she left it behind it would mean that Quintus Tiverton would have to expend more money than he could afford on dressing her for their adventure.

"I will take it with me," Selina told herself.

But she could not prevent a little shudder as she saw that it was torn near the shoulder where the Marquis had clutched at her and she had been forced to struggle free of him.

The cloak which contained her clothes looked a formidably large bundle, when there was a knock on the door and Quintus Tiverton entered the room.

"Are you ready?" he asked in a low voice.

Selina expected him to say that she was bringing too much with her, but he merely glanced at the bundle lying on the floor and said over his shoulder:

"Can you manage this, Jim?"

A small, wiry little man with a lined face and shrewd eyes came in from the landing.

He touched his forelock to Selina and Quintus Tiverton said:

"I have explained to Jim that you are travelling with us, and that you are my sister."

Looking at the servant, Selina felt that he was to be trusted.

Without saying anything he picked up her cloak from the floor, put it under his arm, and preceded them down the stairs.

Every footfall they made seemed to Selina to be so loud that she fancied they must awaken the other occupants in the Inn, and perhaps Mrs. Devilin would come to the door to see what was occurring.

But they reached the Hall without mishap, and the Landlord bowed them out so obsequiously that Selina was certain that Quintus Tiverton must have paid him well and included her bill with his.

In the yard there were three horses already saddled and being held by ostlers.

Selina looked at Quintus Tiverton enquiringly.

"I have hired a horse for you," he explained. "It is the best the Landlord could procure. As long as it will get you there, there will be no reason to complain."

"No, indeed," Selina answered, "and thank you very much."

She half expected that she might have to travel pillion with him or his servant and, seated on the saddle, she lifted the reins with a feeling of delight.

She was sure the horse was as good as, if not better than, those she had been obliged to ride during the last years of her father's life, when he had been economising on horse-flesh as on everything else.

They set off in the morning sunshine and only when they were several miles from the Inn did Quintus Tiverton suggest that they should stop for breakfast.

"I knew that you would wish to get away as quickly as possible," he said, "but I am hungry, and I am sure you are. I fancy you did not eat a very large dinner last night."

Selina flashed him a glance as if she appreciated his understanding, and he thought how incredibly lovely she looked.

He had been half afraid that her beauty had been an illusion of the candle-light, but in the clear morning sunshine she was even more lovely than he remembered.

It was almost impossible, he told himself, for a woman to have a clearer or a more translucent skin. Her hair was the gold of the dawn and her eyes, as he had thought the night before, were exactly the blue of the gentians growing up the slopes of the Alps.

He told himself with a feeling of satisfaction that she would not be long on his hands.

She wanted marriage, which limited the field a little. But if she changed her mind when they reached Baden-Baden, there would be, Quintus Tiverton was convinced, hundreds of men only too willing to lay their fortunes at her feet and offer her their protection.

They had breakfast in a small *Gaus-Haus* where the food was simple but good, and the huge cups of coffee had large clots of thick cream swimming in the centre of them.

"Will you tell me about yourself?" Selina asked. "If we do meet any of your friends I must not make mistakes."

"My father——or rather ours," Quintus Tiverton replied, "was General the Honourable Sir Henry Tiverton, who was decorated for bravery in the field of battle and commanded the Grenadier Guards. He died last year, and my mother three years earlier."

There was a note in his voice as he spoke of his mother which made Selina feel that he did not wish to talk about her, so she asked quickly:

"Where is your home?"

"In Kent," Quintus Tiverton replied. "It is a small Manor House with three hundred acres of land adjoining a large Estate."

There was a different note in his voice now and it seemed to Selina to be one of anger.

She glanced at him a little apprehensively before she said:

"Is there . . . anything else I should . . . know?"

"I think it is unlikely that anyone will cross-question you," Quintus Tiverton replied. "However, if they do, our story is that you have been at a Seminary for Young Ladies in Paris, and I am taking you home, but we decided to visit Baden-Baden on the way."

"By a somewhat round-about route," Selina said with a smile.

"It is what anyone would expect who knows my reputation," Quintus Tiverton replied.

"Why are you a gambler?" she enquired.

"Because I need the money."

"There must be . . . other ways of obtaining it."

"If there are, I am not qualified to practise them," he answered abruptly.

Again, Selina thought that it was a subject about which he did not wish to converse.

He paid the bill and once again they set off. Selina was entranced by the beauty of the countryside; the dark, romantic Black Forest seemed filled with the mythical fair-tale beings she had read of in her books.

They turned a corner where the road was descending sharply downwards and below them they saw that something untoward was happening.

Quintus Tiverton reined in his horse. In the distance they could see a very smart open carriage. It was pulled across the highway, the horses plunging and rearing as if with fright, the coachman tugging at the reins.

There were men in tattered clothing at the sides of the carriage, and even as they stared a shot rang out and a man inside the vehicle toppled backwards.

"Brigands!" Quintus Tiverton ejaculated, and pulling two pistols from his saddle he said to his servant:

"Shall we rush them, Jim?"

"That'd be best, Sir," Jim answered laconically.

"Stay here, Selina," Quintus Tiverton ordered.

Before she could protest, he and Jim spurred their horses forward and started galloping down the hill towards the carriage, shouting at the tops of their voices.

Quintus Tiverton fired one shot at a man with a gun in his hand who was standing beside the carriage. He fell to the ground and almost immediately the rest of the bandits panicked.

They scattered and, running into the shelter of the trees, had disappeared before Quintus Tiverton and Jim reached the carriage.

Quintus Tiverton fired another shot in the direction in which they had gone, as a warning, and then he turned to the occupants of the carriage.

A fashionably gowned and very attractive-looking woman with a piquant face and large, dark eyes exclaimed in French:

"*Grâce à Dieu, Monsieur*, you have arrived! Those devils have wounded le Duc d'Aumale."

Quintus Tiverton alighted from his horse and stepped into the carriage where the Duc was lying back against the cushions clasping his injured arm.

The blood was already soaking over his super-fine

jacket, but he was admirably composed and managed to say with commendable bravery:

"Never have I felt so impotent without a weapon of any sort with which to protect a lady."

"If we can get your coat off, Sire," Quintus Tiverton said, "we can at least stop the flow of blood until you can reach a Surgeon."

"How could we have imagined that so near the town there would be robbers of that sort?" the lady exclaimed as Quintus Tiverton started to divest the Duc of his jacket.

"Have they taken anything valuable?" he asked.

"They had demanded my jewellery and any money we possessed," she replied, "and when the Duc argued with them they shot him."

She gave a sound which was almost a little sob.

"Oh, Henri, I would have been willing to give them everything I possessed rather than that you should suffer."

"Fortunately, Léonide, this gentleman has spared you the making of such a sacrifice," the Duc replied.

Quintus Tiverton glanced at the lady as he rolled back the blood-soaked sleeve of the Duc's shirt.

"I thought I recognised you, Madame," he said, with just a touch of amusement in his voice. "We last met in Paris at a party given by the Marquise de Prava in her fabulous Mansion in the Champs Élysées."

"But of course, I thought your face was familiar!" the lady exclaimed. "You are English and that evening you were with Cora Pearl."

"I was indeed," Quintus Tiverton said, "and you are the famous Madame Léonide Leblanc, and may I say how much I have enjoyed seeing you act some years ago at the *Théâtre des Variétés*."

"I am flattered that you remember me as an actress," Madame Leblanc smiled, but before Quintus Tiverton could reply, Selina came riding up to the carriage.

She had seen what had happened, and now, having ridden slowly forward, she looked a little apprehensively at the dead man lying on the ground.

The footman who had run to the horses' heads when

the catastrophe had occurred had now got the frightened animals under control.

The Duc, concerned though he was with his wound,
which had driven the colour from his face, saw Selina
first.

"You are accompanied by a lady, *Monsieur?*" he
asked.

There was only a faint pause before Quintus Tiverton replied:

"My sister. May I present—Miss Selina Tiverton—
Madame Léonide Leblanc and His Royal Highness le
Duc d'Aumale."

Selina inclined her head, a little embarrassed by such
high-sounding names, but Madame Leblanc exclaimed:

"Your sister! You are bringing her to Baden-
Baden?"

"I am actually taking her back to England," Quintus
Tiverton replied. "She has been at school in Paris, but I
could not resist showing her first the most fashionable
city in Europe, and she is fortunate at this moment to
meet the most beautiful woman in France."

Madame Leblanc gave a musical little laugh.

"You flatter me, *Monsieur*," she said, "but your
lovely sister will certainly not be eclipsed by *les jeunes
femmes* who frequent the Casino."

"Thank you," Quintus Tiverton said, while Selina
blushed and looked quite adorably confused.

Quintus Tiverton had tied a couple of handkerchiefs
round the Duc's arm to prevent it from bleeding and
now placed his jacket over his shoulders and said:

"You must hurry, Sire, to a proper Surgeon who will
extract the bullet. There is no need for me to tell you
that you are very fortunate in receiving only a flesh-
wound. Had the bandits shot you in the chest, it might
have been exceedingly dangerous."

"You are only making me more ashamed of myself
than I am already," the Duc answered, "for escorting
Madame without providing her with proper protection.
Never again will I venture outside Baden-Baden without a pistol and outriders."

"It is a wise precaution," Quintus Tiverton agreed.
"As you well know, stories of the fortunes won at the

tables and the jewels of the beautiful women lose nothing in their telling. There are always those willing to pick the plums from a rich man's pocket."

As he spoke he stepped down from the coach, and Madame Leblanc bent forward and held out her hand.

"How can we thank you, Monsieur Tiverton?" she asked. "We are both deeply in your debt."

"I hope you will allow me to call on you," Quintus Tiverton said as he kissed her hand.

"You know we should be very offended if you did not do so," Madame Leblanc answered. "I shall expect you this evening, informally, and then we must make plans to entertain you and your charming sister—if she will come."

There was just a little pause before the last three words, and Quintus Tiverton knew exactly what she meant before he replied:

"My sister and I would be honoured to see you again, Madame."

Again he kissed her hand, and then the carriage drove away, Madame Leblanc waving her hand as it did so, but the Duc's eyes were on Selina.

Quintus Tiverton stood for a moment watching the carriage until it was out of sight and then he looked down at the dead bandit.

"See if there is anything of value on him, Jim," he said. "It would be a pity for his friends to enjoy his ill-gotten gains."

Jim, who had been holding his Master's horse as well as his own, gave Quintus Tiverton the bridles and bent over the bandit.

The bullet which had killed him had entered his body exactly over the heart and his shirt was already stained with blood. Selina turned her head as Jim searched the man's pockets and opened the small haversack he carried over his shoulder.

"Several thousand francs, Sir, two gold watches, and a dozen rings," he said.

"We will leave the jewellery at the Town Hall," Quintus Tiverton replied. "There will doubtless be a reward for them. The money is not worth mentioning."

"No, of course not, Sir."

The two men mounted their horses and rode on.

"Who was that lady?" Selina asked.

It seemed to her that Quintus Tiverton hesitated for a moment before he replied:

"Madame Léonide Leblanc made her name as an actress when she was little more than a child, and has often performed in Paris. She has travelled in many parts of the world and she is an extremely successful gambler."

He paused to add impressively:

"They say that in Hamburg her total winnings were over half a million!"

Selina gave an exclamation of surprise and Quintus Tiverton went on:

"Twice at Baden-Baden she has broken the bank, but money runs through her fingers like water."

"She is very attractive," Selina said in a low voice.

"That is what the Duc thinks."

"They are engaged to be married?"

Quintus Tiverton smiled at the naivety of it.

"No, indeed, but it is a very important liaison, and Madame Leblanc's sumptuous apartment in the Boulevard Haussman contains bibelots and objets d'art which are the envy of all Paris."

"You . . . mean," Selina said in a low voice, "that Madame Leblanc . . . is the Duc's . . . mistress?"

"Does that shock you?"

"N-no," Selina answered a little uncertainly, "but she is so beautiful, so elegant, it seems strange that she should not be married."

"She has been married," Quintus Tiverton replied. "I believe her husband was a German photographer, but most conveniently he vanished."

He saw the puzzled expression on Selina's face and almost hated himself because he had not lied about Madame Leblanc and let her remain in ignorance.

Then he told himself almost savagely that Selina would have to grow up sooner or later and there was a great deal more about Léonide Leblanc which he could have said.

Witty, piquant, very ambitious and amusing, she was

amongst *la guade*, the dozen most famous courtesans in Paris.

Unlike the majority of them, she was also extremely good-natured and noted for many instances of kindness. She was however nicknamed by the men-about-town, or *noceurs*, "Mademoiselle Maximum."

Perhaps this referred to her fees or accomplishments, but more probably to the number of her lovers.

As one Frenchman had remarked to Quintus Tiverton:

"Léonide is a modern Ninon de Lenclos. But, my dear fellow, if you put her on top of Mont Blanc, she would still be accessible!"

Quintus Tiverton was well aware that le Duc d'Aumale, Grand Seigneur of Chantilly, the fourth son of King Louis Philippe, was more important than any of her previous protectors and completely infatuated with her.

He was a great gentleman and under his protection Léonide could entertain the most distinguished men in France and those with the most intelligence.

It might harm Selina socially, Quintus Tiverton decided, to be seen in the company of Léonide Leblanc, but she would undoubtedly meet men who would not submit to the boredom of more respectable houses.

He was also well aware that the aristocratic socialites would not welcome in their midst, however well born, someone as beautiful as Selina with apparently no other assets.

As they rode on towards Baden-Baden he decided that nothing could be more useful than the fact that he had put not only Léonide Leblanc but also the Duc d'Aumale under an obligation to him before they had even arrived at their destination.

He had already decided that they should stay the first night at the Hotel Stephanie-les-Bains. It was the oldest and most important Hotel in Baden-Baden. It was also the most expensive, and Quintus Tiverton was well aware that he had very little ready money.

But the Casino was waiting for him and, like all gamblers, he was convinced that once he was seated at

the green baize tables, luck would favour him as it had
done in the past.

Selina was very quiet as they rode into the attractive
old town. She was thinking of Madame Léonide Leblanc and wondering how she could compete with a
woman whose eyes seemed to sparkle more brightly
than her jewels and whose appearance was so finished,
so sophisticated, so chic that she was sure that in her
presence she would always appear gauche and insignificant.

'Supposing,' she thought, 'no-one ever notices me
and Mr. Tiverton finds me heavy on his hands?'

She shivered as she anticipated how ashamed she
would be to have to batten on his generosity and spend
his money, after forcing herself upon him against his
instinct to leave her where she was.

"I must learn to be attractive," Selina told herself pathetically. "How can I make myself charming and fascinating like the lady in the carriage?"

It seemed to her a hopeless task and when finally
they were shown to their rooms in the Hotel Stephanie
and their small amount of luggage was carried upstairs,
she looked despairingly at the white gown.

It was creased and crumpled after the manner in
which it had been packed, and Selina thought that after
all she should have spent the money Quintus Tiverton
had offered her in buying her ticket back to England.

She had however little time for introspection, for as
soon as they arrived Quintus Tiverton was giving orders—a dress-maker, a *coiffeur*, a tailor, a shoe-maker,
and glove-maker were summoned to their bed-chambers.

These were communicating rooms on the second
floor. Quintus Tiverton had asked for the best, but the
Hotel was full and those on the first floor were all engaged.

"The luggage will be coming later," he had said on
their arrival, in a lofty voice. "The train from Paris was
held up by a fall of stone and my sister and I decided
to ride here rather than wait interminably for the line
to be cleared."

"These delays are always happening, *Mein Herr*," the manager of the Stephanie said sympathetically.

"In the meantime, we must repair our wardrobes."

Quintus Tiverton spoke with a grandeur that commanded respect in the Hotel, and it appeared to Selina that everyone ran to do his bidding.

Almost before she had unpacked the things wrapped up in her cloak, the dress-maker had arrived and Quintus Tiverton was ordering such a large number of gowns that she gasped.

She tried to persuade him that he must not be so extravagant, but it was difficult to do so in front of the dress-maker.

"I will buy only what I can have immediately," Quintus Tiverton said in fluent German which sounded even more authoritative than if he had spoken in French.

"My girls will work all night, *Mein Herr*," the dress-maker assured him. "They are most of them French and come from Paris, so they are very skilled."

Materials were produced, satins, lamés, gauzes, tulles, velvets. Sketches were altered or redrawn and finally an order which ran into an exorbitant amount of money was given. The dress-maker, overwhelmed by such patronage, curtseyed her way from the room.

Selina was about to say that it was impossible for her to accept so many things, but Quintus Tiverton had already gone to where a tailor was waiting for him.

The *coiffeur* recommended by the Hotel arranged Selina's hair, the chamber-maid took away her white dress to press and mend it, and in a quicker space of time than she could have believed possible she was ready.

Looking as elegant and fashionable as she had done two evenings before when she had gone downstairs in Paris and encountered the Marquis, she stared at her reflection in a mirror.

The maid was putting the last finishing touches to her gown when there was a knock on the communicating door between her bed-room and Quintus Tiverton's.

"May I come in?" he asked in English.

"I am ready," Selina replied.

He entered and she waited apprehensively, wondering if he would approve of how she looked, or think perhaps that there was something wrong.

She had in fact with the help of the chamber-maid managed to insert a small amount of tulle in the décolletage of the gown.

It was now far more modest and Selina told herself severely that she should never have worn it as it was. She might have known that no-one respectable would have appeared in anything so daring.

Quintus Tiverton stood inside the door and looked her over.

If Selina looked very different from the girl he had seen crying on the bed in her night-gown, or riding beside him in an unfashionable English habit, she on looking at him was positively overcome!

He had been extremely attractive in his riding-clothes, but in evening-dress she thought him overwhelming!

The spotless elegance of his stiff white shirt and white tie and the close-fitting, long-tailed evening-coat made him seem taller and even more impressive than he had been before.

The fear flashed through Selina's mind that he might leave her at home because she was not smart enough to accompany him.

Then he smiled and said in a voice which she found most beguiling:

"I have no doubt that a great number of men I have never met before will claim acquaintance with me this evening after they have seen my pretty sister."

"I look . . . all right?" Selina asked.

"You look very beautiful," he answered. "That is what you want to hear, is it not?"

"Only if it is the . . . truth."

"I think you and I must agree always to be truthful to each other," Quintus Tiverton replied. "I should in fact have remembered to make it part of our bargain."

The maid had withdrawn tactfully at his entrance, and now Selina said:

"You are quite sure that I will not shame you? If

you would rather I stayed here alone until my new gowns arrive tomorrow, I will do so."

Quintus Tiverton looked at her.

"Look in the mirror, Selina! There is no need for me to tell you what you can see for yourself."

"I feel . . . shy."

He smiled at her.

"Come, I think this is the beginning of our adventure, the first step forward, and neither of us knows what lies ahead!"

It was difficult for Selina afterwards to remember everything that happened. It was all so exciting.

They had dined in the large Dining-Room of the Hotel, which looked out over a garden which was bordered by the little River Oos running beside the beautiful Lichentaler Allee down which the carriages drove in the day-time.

It was however too late for Selina to see much that evening, and she was frantically hungry after their long ride and the fact that they had lunched very lightly.

The food she ate was delicious and included what Quintus Tiverton told her were amongst the specialties of the Black Forest: deer paté and a soft creamy cheesecake, besides too many other dishes for Selina to remember.

"Tomorrow," he said, "you shall eat Rosenküchen."

"Rose-cakes?" Selina translated.

"Or, if you prefer, eels and frogs' legs," he teased, and laughed as she shuddered.

Because Selina was so interested he told her how Baden-Baden had been a Spa since 125 A.D., when it was known as Aurelia Aquensis.

Roman soldiers had recovered their health by drinking and bathing in the waters, and in the Middle-Ages three thousand guests a year had come to take a cure.

"Is there a King of Baden?" Selina asked.

"It is an independent country, governed by the Margrave of Baden and the Dukes of Zachringen," Quintus Tiverton replied. "It is, incidentally, one of the oldest Dynasties in Europe. The Margrave was offered and refused a Royal Crown, but he accepted the title of the Grand Duke of Baden."

"Shall I see them?" Selina enquired, with a childish desire to look at Royalty.

"They will doubtless be at the races," Quintus Tiverton replied, "which are very fashionable and rather like the Royal Ascot Race Meeting in England."

There were so many things he told Selina that she found interesting and as they finished their dinner she said:

"I have loved everything you have talked to me about. Do you realise that except for the night when I dined with the Marquis, I have never before dined with a gentleman alone?"

"I wish I could have been the first," Quintus Tiverton replied, "but I am delighted to have been your second choice."

"It was not my . . . choice, as you well . . . know," Selina answered.

"Forget it," he said as he saw a cloud overshadow the happiness on her face. "Forget everything that happened until we met. If you are acting a part, it is always wisest to think yourself into it."

"That is what I am trying to do," Selina said, "to think myself into being your . . . sister."

As she said the words she looked up at him and their eyes met. There was an expression in his which she did not understand. Then as she looked at him enquiringly he said:

"Come, we must go to the Casino. I forgot to tell you that I did not visit Madame Leblanc this evening, as she asked me. Instead I received a message inviting us both to have supper later with her and the Duc at his Villa. I am sure you will enjoy that."

"Yes, of course," Selina answered.

At the same time she could not help feeling that she would much rather have had supper alone with Quintus Tiverton.

A carriage drove them the short distance to the Casino, which looked like a classical Temple outside and, although Selina did not realise it, like the Palace of Versailles within.

There were statues of goddesses holding huge candelabra on their heads, and there was a white room furnished in Louis XVI style with gold lattice-work and arabesques.

There was the Pompadour Salon, which had been copied from Madame Pompadour's room in the Trianon, and the Green Room in the Renaissance style of Louis XIII.

It was all very ornate, luxurious, and bewildering, and it was with difficulty that Selina did not hold tightly on to Quintus Tiverton's arm for fear that she should lose him.

Far more impressive than the Casino itself were the people it contained. Never had she imagined that there could be so many ultra-fashionable persons congregated in so small a space.

The men were distinguished. In fact, as she was to learn later, they bore the most honoured and noble names in Europe and Russia. The women were breathtaking.

Their gowns, embroidered, feathered, be-flowered, draped, looped, pleated, be-ribboned, and fringed, all vied with one another in a kaleidoscope of colour.

But if their gowns were sensational, they were nothing in comparision with their jewels. It seemed almost impossible that long white necks and slim arms should carry such a fortune in gems without being exhausted by the weight of them.

Selina was conscious of feeling almost naked amidst such a glittering profusion of diamonds, sapphires, rubies, and emeralds. She had no idea that in fact she stood out like a lily in a Conservatory filled with exotic orchids.

Quintus Tiverton led Selina slowly towards the gaming-tables and, as he had anticipated, there seemed a large number of men ready to claim his acquaintance.

As one stopped to talk to him, so two or three others came up to be introduced. But as he shook them by the hand their eyes were on Selina.

"My sister!" He must have repeated the two words a hundred times until as if he could not restrain himself he said to Selina:

"I want to gamble. Come and stand behind me and endeavour to understand the game."

Selina did as she was told and saw the gold coins arranged in piles along the edge of the table and fingers that gripped them fervently like claws.

For the first time she watched men and women concentrating on a game of chance and realised the intensity of their emotions as they won or lost money.

At the beginning of the game she was afraid that Quintus Tiverton would lose. She was well aware that since they had arrived in Baden-Baden he was already deeply in debt.

There was the Hotel accommodation to be paid, the gowns he had ordered for her, and the suits for himself. At dinner they had been served with a golden wine which Quintus Tiverton had described as being a "special vintage."

"What will happen if he loses?" Selina asked herself.

Her fingers gripped the back of his chair until with an inexpressible feeling of relief she saw the pile of gold coins in front of him increasing.

She had the feeling that while he played he had forgotten her very existence.

In fact, when one of the gentlemen to whom she had already been introduced came to her side she was certain that Quintus Tiverton did not hear their conversation.

"May I get you a drink, *Mademoiselle?*" the Frenchman asked.

"No, thank you," Selina replied, "I am watching my brother."

"Shall I explain the game," he enquired, "or are you already aware of the rules?"

"It is all completely bewildering to me."

"Let me be your teacher," he said. "Come with me to the next table."

A little reluctantly but feeling that perhaps it was rude to refuse, Selina let him lead her to where Roulette was being played.

She stood watching the little white ball bouncing up and down, and money being swept away from those who had staked their gold on the wrong number, while

her escort explained rather ponderously the odds that
were paid on single numbers or combinations.

Then as the croupier cried:

"*Faites vos jeux, Messieurs et Mesdames,*" Selina
said:

"I am certain twenty-nine will come up this time!"

"Then we must back it," her teacher said quickly.

He put several gold pieces on the number even as
Selina put out her hand to stop him.

"I may be . . . wrong," she protested.

Before he could reply, the croupier's voice rang out:

"*Vingt neuf—noir, impair et passe.*"

"I was right!" Selina exclaimed.

"They say that a lovely woman always wins the first
time she plays. It is a tradition," the Frenchman smiled.

When the stake was paid he swept the pile of golden
coins from the table and put them into Selina's hands.

"They are not . . . mine!" she said.

"It was your bet," he answered.

"But I cannot accept these, *Monsieur*," she said
quickly. "It was your money you risked."

"On your inspiration!"

"No, please," Selina pleaded. "I could not think of
taking all this!"

She spoke so earnestly that the Frenchman said:

"Anyone can see, *Mademoiselle*, that you are not
used to Casinos. But if it will please you, I will take
back the money I staked, on condition that you tell me
on which number I should now place a bet."

"I would be . . . afraid to try . . . again," Selina faltered.

"Please try," the Frenchman begged.

Selina had no bag in which to place her money so,
still holding it in her hands although it was rather cum-
bersome, she stood watching the roulette ball nervously.

She had been so sure that number twenty-nine was
going to come up. Could she possibly be sure a second
time?

"*Faites vos jeux, Messieurs et Mesdames.*"

The croupier's voice was expressionless and now he

spun the ball. Just as he was about to speak again Selina said:

"*Sept.*"

The Frenchman bent forward and his money was on the table even as the croupier cried:

"*Rien ne va plus!*"

There was a pause and he added:

"*Sept—rouge, impair et manque.*"

Selina had won for the second time, and she looked at the man beside her with shining eyes.

"Now I have paid you back."

"You must try again," he insisted.

Selina shook her head.

"No, I am sure it would be unlucky. I am not a gambler. I must go and tell my brother what has happened."

She turned from her escort's side without waiting for him to collect his gains and hurried back to where she had left Quintus Tiverton.

As she reached him he was just rising from the table.

"Look what I have won!" she said excitedly. "Will you take it?"

She put the gold into his hands and as she did so looked up at his face.

"You . . . lost!" she said in a voice that was little above a whisper.

"I lost," he replied.

"Then this will bring you luck," Selina said. "I am sure of it! I feel it, just as I knew what number was about to turn up on the Roulette-Table."

"Do you mean that?" Quintus Tiverton asked. "It is your money, Selina."

"Do you really expect me to keep it for myself," she asked, "when I owe you more than I can ever repay?"

He looked at her and then he said quickly:

"No, I do not think you would do that. May I play with your money, Selina?"

"It is yours," she said softly, "and it will bring you luck."

Quintus Tiverton took the coins from her and walked across the room.

Selina followed him.

They were just about to go into the Blue Room, where Baccarat was in progress, when a man exclaimed:

"Hello, Tiverton, I might have expected to find you here. Are you winning?"

"On the contrary," Quintus Tiverton replied.

"Oh, well, lucky at cards—unlucky in love," the man remarked and he was looking at Selina.

"May I introduce my sister?" Quintus Tiverton asked. "You will think it rude, but I have forgotten your name."

"Wilton. We met last in Cairo, if you remember."

"But of course," Quintus Tiverton said. "Selina, may I introduce Sir John Wilton, a very gallant soldier!"

"I am out of the Army now," Sir John said. "Will you come and have a drink with me?"

"I have an urgent desire to play Baccarat," Quintus Tiverton replied, "but I would be grateful if you could look after my sister for a short while. I do not like her standing about alone."

"No, of course not," Sir John said. "Let us sit down, Miss Tiverton. I have a feeling this is your first visit to a Casino."

"Why should you think that?" Selina enquired.

"I can give you the answer, but it will take a little time," Sir John replied.

He did in fact say a great many flattering things to Selina, but she could give him only half her attention, for all the time she was thinking about Quintus Tiverton and willing him to win.

She was sure that the money she had given him would bring him luck, just as she had known what number would turn up at Roulette.

'Perhaps later,' she thought, 'he will stand beside me and I can win for him as I did for the Frenchman.'

Then she remembered how Sir John had said:

"Lucky at cards—unlucky in love."

Was Quintus Tiverton lucky in love? She knew so little about him. Who was Cora Pearl, with whom he had been in Paris when he had met Madame Leblanc?

Was she perhaps a beautiful actress, or had she been Quintus Tiverton's mistress?

Selina did not understand why it gave her a funny little pain in her heart to think of him with a beautiful mistress.

There must, she thought, have been many women in his life because he was so attractive; so kind; so wonderful in every way!

He had said that he was "hard-hearted," but who else would have helped her escape from Mrs. Devilin, brought her here with him to Baden-Baden, and been prepared to find her a husband?

It was frightening to think that that was what she had to do. At the same time she knew she could not let Quintus Tiverton down.

He had made her promise that she must accept a man once he had found one for her, and suddenly she wondered if Sir John Wilton might be the person they were seeking.

She turned to look at him with wide eyes as if she saw him for the first time.

"You are lovely! Exquisitely lovely!" Sir John said, "but too many men must have told you that already."

Selina shook her head.

"Then let me repeat what I have just said," Sir John went on. "You are unbelievably beautiful, Miss Tiverton, so beautiful that I am concerned your brother should have brought you to a place like this."

"Why not?" Selina asked.

"Because I think you should be in the Ball-Rooms of London, at the Receptions given by the great English hostesses, in the more sedate atmosphere of Buckingham Palace."

Selina gave a little laugh.

"I am not likely to be invited to any of those places."

"Why not?" Sir John enquired.

"Well . . . for one thing, I am quite sure my brother could not afford it."

She had been about to say that she was not important enough, when she remembered who she was supposed to be.

Sir John looked surprised.

"Is the Earl keeping him short?" he asked. "Oh,

well, it is not surprising. I suppose Arkley hates your brother. It is understandable, but he is a hard man."

It was all bewildering to Selina as she wondered who the Earl was, remembering that Quintus Tiverton had only spoken of his father and mother.

"Where are you staying in Baden-Baden, Sir John?" she asked, intent upon changing the conversation.

"My wife and I are the guests of the Margrave," Sir John replied. "It is always rather boring at their Castle and I managed to escape after dinner. Now that I have met you I am very glad indeed that I did so."

Selina gave a little sigh of relief.

One thing was quite certain: Quintus Tiverton would not expect her to marry Sir John.

Chapter Four

Quintus Tiverton returned from the Baccarat-Room to find Selina and Sir John.

She glanced at him quickly and apprehensively, hoping he had won. But his face was quite expressionless and she told herself that a real gambler would never reveal any emotion where his gaming was concerned.

They were sitting talking with Sir John Wilton and Quintus was drinking wine when there was a considerable commotion at the end of the room.

Selina saw a woman resplendently gowned and covered in diamonds moving slowly across the Salon on the arm of a very distinguished-looking man with a small Imperial beard.

"Caroline Letessier!" Quintus Tiverton said almost as if he spoke to himself.

"I thought she was in Russia," Sir John remarked.

"His Imperial Highness is with her, so I imagine they have returned," Quintus Tiverton said dryly.

It was difficult to imagine that anyone could wear so many diamonds simultaneously. Caroline Letessier literally glittered like one of the crystal chandeliers hanging over her head.

"She has been away for eight years," Quintus Tiverton remarked, "and yet she looks very little different from when she appeared at the Théâtre du Palais-Royal."

"You are right," Sir John agreed. "I remember her well from my bachelor days. I thought then that she had more charm than any other woman in Paris, and of course she was extremely intelligent."

By now Caroline Letessier's entrance had been gen-

erally observed and young men were hurrying across
the Casino almost to encircle her.

"Let us go and pay our respects to the Grand
Duke," Sir John suggested.

Selina was delighted at the chance to see the diamonds closer than she could from where they were sitting.

They moved across the Salon to find by the time
they reached the distinguished couple that it was almost
impossible to get near them.

Everyone appeared to be chattering at the tops of
their voices, not only in French and English but also in
German.

Caroline Letessier was responding with a wit and a
gaiety which made every word she said seem to sparkle.

She had, Selina noticed, a spontaneous grace and a
highly expressive face, while her smile was remarkably
alluring.

"She really is absolutely unchanged!" she heard Sir
John say to Quintus Tiverton.

"I agree with you," he replied, "and I would recog-
nise those multi-coloured jewelled butterflies strewn in
her black hair if I saw them anywhere in the world."

Sir John laughed.

"I wonder if she still has the golden apple in which
she kept her rice-powder, and which she always arranged on the plush-covered ledge of her stage-box?"

"Accompanying it was her mirror, her lorgnette set
with diamonds," Quintus Tiverton said. "In fact everything about her was always elegant."

"Paris must have missed her," Sir John smiled. "Let
us hope that now she has returned from St. Petersburg
she intends to stay."

"Eight years is a long time," Quintus Tiverton said
reflectively.

As he spoke Caroline Letessier saw him and she
gave a little cry of delight.

"Quintus!" she exclaimed, "how delightful to see you
here."

The encircling *jeunesse dorée* opened their ranks to

allow Quintus Tiverton to reach her and he raised both
her hands to his lips.

"May I say how delighted we are to welcome you
home?" he asked.

"Not half as delighted as we are to be back."

"We have heard so many stories about you. You
must have been a great success," Quintus Tiverton
went on, "but Russia's gain was our sad loss."

The Grand Duke, who had been speaking to someone else, now held out his hand.

"It is good to see you, Tiverton."

"You take the very words from my mouth, your Imperial Highness," Quintus Tiverton replied.

"We arrived only yesterday," the Grand Duke said,
"and this is our first appearance in the Casino. You see
before you 'Monsieur et Madame Letessier,' and that is
how we intend to be known."

Everyone laughed, but at that moment Hortense
Schneider, an actress who had had so many Royal lovers that she was known as *"le passage des Princes,"* exclaimed in a loud voice that was perfectly audible to
everyone surrounding Caroline Letessier:

"I have seen fatted calves in my time, but never such
a pretty one as this!"

There was a moment's pregnant silence and then in a
sharp staccato voice Caroline Letessier replied acidly:

"And I have never seen such an ugly cow!"

There was immediately an uproar in which everyone
spoke at once.

Some gentlemen demanded satisfaction from Lord
Carrington, who was escorting Hortense Schneider, others appealed to the Grand Duke, who stood looking extremely angry but saying little.

There was so much noise that the Director of the
Casino came up to investigate.

By this time rival factions were insisting that either
Caroline Letessier or Hortense Schneider should be
asked to leave the Casino. But before the Director
could speak, the Grand Duchess of Baden's son rose
from one of the tables.

Crossing the room, he raised Caroline Letessier's
hand to his lips and said:

"Beauty and wit are things which have been lamentably lacking in Baden until you arrived."

Then offering Caroline Letessier his arm, he led her towards the Roulette-Table, leaving those who had opposed her looking foolish and somewhat shame-facedly apologetic.

"Why did that woman say that?" Selina asked Quintus Tiverton in a low voice.

She was intensely curious. She had never expected ladies who were so elegantly dressed and so splendidly bejewelled to behave in such a vulgar manner.

"Caroline Letessier's foster-father was a butcher," Quintus Tiverton replied. "Although she has been fêted by some of the greatest men in Paris, acted in the Théâtre Michel in St. Petersburg, and has completely captivated the Grand Duke, she has not forgotten her humble origins."

He laughed.

"It still makes her annoyed to be reminded of them."

Selina thought it was very strange that despite the splendid appearance of such women, despite the fact that they were escorted by such distinguished gentlemen, they could in fact behave like fish-wives.

When she looked at Hortense Schneider it was to realise that she wore nearly as many jewels as Caroline Letessier.

It was even stranger, she thought to herself, that women who came from such humble origins should manage to collect so much wealth.

It was also extraordinary that Quintus Tiverton should know them all so well!

She was to find herself thinking that again later in the evening when they arrived at the Duc d'Aumale's Villa for supper.

It was after midnight before they left the Casino, and when they were in the carriage Selina could not help asking the question that was uppermost in her mind.

"Did I bring you . . . luck?" she asked.

She thought that Quintus Tiverton hesitated for a moment before he replied:

"The answer is yes, although I do not like discussing my losses or gains."

"I know I should not have asked," Selina replied, "but I am so curious."

She paused for a moment and then went on:

"It was so exciting when *vingt-neuf* turned up and then number seven!"

"Your Frenchman friend was very impressed by your clairvoyance," Quintus Tiverton said dryly. "He sat next to me later at the Baccarat-Table and told me of your predictions."

"Was it wrong of me," Selina asked, "to accept the money from him as he insisted?"

"I should think you very foolish if you had not done so," Quintus Tiverton answered. "In fact, you were extremely generous to allow him to keep all he had won on the second number."

There was something in his voice which made Selina feel that she had behaved stupidly.

After a moment she said:

"But surely it would not have been . . . right for me to accept . . . money from a strange man?"

"Right?" Quintus Tiverton queried. "It is difficult to know where right ends and wrong begins when it means the difference between eating or going hungry."

Selina thought about this for a moment and then she said:

"Knowing how much you have . . . spent on me, I now see that it was . . . foolish of me not to accept anything he might have been . . . prepared to . . . give me."

There was silence, and then Quintus Tiverton said almost as if the words were forced from him:

"No! You were right, of course you were right! It is only that I find myself worrying, Selina, how I can look after you properly. I have had only myself to trouble about in the past."

The candle-lantern which lit the inside of the carriage revealed his face and Selina glanced at him apprehensively.

"I am . . . sorry to be such a . . . burden."

"I daresay it will not be for long," he replied almost sharply. "You certainly made an impression in the Casino tonight. I was inundated with invitations to parties. I did not deceive myself by believing it was on account of my own popularity."

Selina hesitated and then she said:

"I am ... glad that you were not ... ashamed of me."

"Did you really imagine it was possible I might be?" Quintus Tiverton asked in a strange voice.

Before Selina could reply the carriage drew up outside the porticoed front door of a very sumptuous Villa situated a little above the town and surrounded by a large garden.

They were announced, to find the Royal Duc seated in an arm-chair, his arm in a sling, while Léonide Leblanc in rustling green silk with a profusion of emeralds was entertaining a large number of guests.

She held out her hands to Quintus Tiverton exclaiming:

"Here is my gallant saviour! I was just telling these gentlemen, Quintus, how those cut-throats fled at your approach despite the fact that they out-numbered you and your servant."

"It was my good fortune to be of service," Quintus Tiverton replied.

Madame Leblanc turned to Selina.

"And I hope you, Miss Tiverton, have recovered from the shock of seeing that bandit dead on the ground and His Royal Highness bleeding from a bullet-wound."

"It must have been very frightening for you, Madame," Selina said in her soft voice. "You were very brave."

"I think we both behaved with commendable courage," Léonide Leblanc replied. "Come, let me introduce you to my friends."

She rattled off a great number of illustrious names, far too many for Selina to remember, but she curtseyed gracefully at every introduction, and as her hostess moved away she found herself surrounded by gentlemen anxious to hear more of the adventure in which she had been involved.

"It is absolutely disgraceful that these murderous

rascals should be allowed to come so near to the town," one of the guests remarked. "I shall take the matter up myself with the Margrave, and he must insist on better protection for the patrons of Baden-Baden."

Everyone seemed to have a story to tell of how they had been accosted in the woods by robbers or how friends had endured much the same experience as Madame Leblanc and the Duc.

While they were talking, Selina could not help noticing how the gentlemen in the Salon out-numbered the ladies by about five to one.

Soon after they arrived Caroline Letessier and the Grand Duke came on from the Casino.

Léonide Leblanc greeted them effusively, and there was no doubt that the Duc d'Aumale was delighted to see his Russian counterpart.

"Why have you returned?" he asked, and Selina, who was standing near the two distinguished men, heard the Grand Duke reply:

"Caroline had been warned for some time that she had out-stayed her welcome in my country. The Tsarina dislikes women who are more beautiful than herself, and certainly those who receive more attention!"

The Duc d'Aumale laughed.

"I should have thought that the fact that Caroline is an actress would have been sufficient to grant her immunity from the attention of the Secret Police."

"Nobody is immune from them!" the Grand Duke replied, and his voice was sharp. "Finally it grew too dangerous for her to remain."

"And you came with her," the Duc d'Aumale remarked with a faint smile on his lips.

"I only just managed to do so," His Imperial Highness replied dryly. "My Uncle sent instructions to Berlin that I was to return to St. Petersburg."

The Duc d'Aumale raised his eye-brows as the Grand Duke continued:

"The Chief of Police tried to demand my return, and when I said to him: 'You would not dare to arrest me,' he replied:

" 'No, Your Imperial Highness, but we can detach

your railway carriage from the train so that it will be impossible for you to travel any further.' "

"Good God!" the Duc d'Aumale exclaimed. "And how did you solve the problem?"

"In the usual way," the Grand Duke answered. "Is there a country in the world where money does not speak louder than words?"

The two gentlemen laughed; but Selina looked at Caroline Letessier and wondered what it was which made her so attractive that a man like the Grand Duke of Russia would risk the displeasure of his Uncle and his Emperor for her charms.

There was no doubt that the Grand Duke was not the only person who found her captivating: Quintus Tiverton was laughing at everything she said.

There was something provocative in her eyes as she looked at him, and Selina could not help thinking with a little pang that her red lips, as they curved in an irresistible smile, were very inviting.

"Why cannot I be like that?" she asked herself almost miserably.

Then her attention was distracted by Madame Leblanc.

"I want to introduce a compatriot of yours, Miss Tiverton," she said. "Lord Howdrith has especially asked to be presented to you."

As Selina sank gracefully in a deep curtsey, she thought that Lord Howdrith was the most English-looking Englishman she had ever seen.

He was tall, fair, and blue-eyed, and had that lazy air of superiority which seemed characteristic of the English.

"Our hostess tells me that you have only just arrived in Baden-Baden," Lord Howdrith said.

His voice too was very English with its slight drawl and cultivated tone, while Selina could not help thinking that the very banality of his words was characteristic.

"Yes, we arrived this afternoon," Selina said, "and as Your Lordship has doubtless heard, were involved in an adventure before we even reached the town."

"It must have been very disturbing," Lord Howdrith remarked.

He turned his head and suggested:

"Shall we sit down? I find it extremely boring, this habit of endlessly standing about. I cannot imagine why foreigners never seem to avail themselves of chairs."

Selina felt that there was nothing she could do but acquiesce, and they moved a little way across the Salon to a velvet-covered sofa set in a corner between two tables massed with exotic hot-house flowers.

"Are you and your brother staying long?" His Lordship enquired.

"I have no idea," Selina replied. "We are on our way back to England."

She was anxious not to be cross-questioned as to where they would go when they reached England in case she should make a mistake; so she said quickly:

"Why are you in Baden-Baden?"

"The reason," Lord Howdrith answered, "is that I have two horses running in the races, both of which I expect to win."

"Do tell me about them," Selina asked.

She found it easy not to pay very close attention to all Lord Howdrith was saying and to watch at the same time what was happening in the main part of the room.

Quintus Tiverton was still at Caroline Letessier's side and, as she raised her face to his, Selina could see the jewelled butterflies glittering in her hair.

Had he loved her in the past? she wondered. Had the vivacious, attractive actress meant something in his life?

She wondered why it hurt her to think of it and made her feel so dissatisfied with her own appearance that she wished they had not come to the party tonight!

Tomorrow she could have worn one of her new gowns which would be more becoming than the one she had on.

Then she knew that she was being hypersensitive.

Never before had she owned such a beautiful dress as she was wearing now, and she doubted somewhat despondently if the gowns that were being made would make her any the less insignificant than she already appeared beside glittering Birds of Paradise like Léonide Leblanc and Caroline Letessier.

No wonder, she told herself, Quintus Tiverton found her an encumbrance and a bore when these were the women with whom he was most at ease.

Ignorant though she was of social life, Selina could not help understanding that distinguished, intelligent, and important men, and beautiful women who were not prudish and strait-laced, were amusing for an unencumbered bachelor.

"Of course this is more fun for him," Selina told herself, "than prim and proper social occasions."

As she thought of it she saw Caroline Letessier kiss Quintus Tiverton's cheek while those round them were laughing at something she had said.

"I asked you, Miss Tiverton," Lord Howdrith was saying, "whether you would permit me to call on you tomorrow, perhaps to take you driving in the Black Forest?"

Selina realised with a start that she had not heard a word he had been saying.

"It is very kind of you," she answered, "but I must first find out what ... plans my brother has ... made."

"I will speak to him myself," Lord Howdrith said. "We were at Eton together, where, as I expect you remember, he distinguished himself on the cricket field."

"Yes, of course," Selina said hastily.

A small orchestra had appeared, which started to play the strains of an Offenbach waltz.

Léonide Leblanc began to dance with Quintus Tiverton and before Lord Howdrith could invite Selina onto the floor, a Frenchman whose name she could not remember asked her to dance.

She accepted and immediately he began to pay her flattering and fulsome compliments.

"You are entrancing!" he said. "You are like a star that has fallen out of the sky! You make all the diamonds seem mundane, flashy, and rather vulgar."

"I think you are being rather rude to our hostess," Selina said demurely.

At the same time there was a note in the Frenchman's voice which made her feel shy.

She could not explain it, any more than she could explain that there was something in his eyes which vaguely reminded her of the Marquis.

"Why have we not met before?" he went on. "Have you come from Paris? I thought I knew every beauty in that city of beautiful women."

"I ... I have been at school there," Selina said quickly, remembering that that was the part she had to play.

"School!" he exclaimed. "That accounts for it! And who has brought you to Baden-Baden?"

"My brother," Selina replied, and saw there was a look of surprise on his face as he said:

"Your brother? Then in that case . . ."

He did not finish the sentence, and Selina felt somehow that it might have been offensive if he had.

She did not know why, but she had no desire to dance with the Frenchman again.

When the music stopped she moved away from him, back to where Lord Howdrith was still sitting, where she had left him, on the sofa.

"Please, *Mademoiselle,* do not leave me," the Frenchman begged. "We must dance again. I cannot allow you to escape."

"If you will excuse me, I would like to rest," Selina answered. "I have had a long day and I am very tired."

She sat down beside Lord Howdrith as she spoke and the Frenchman, somewhat discomfited, moved away.

"Has that bounder been upsetting you?" Lord Howdrith enquired in English.

"Not exactly," Selina replied, "but I find compliments, which I know mean nothing, slightly embarrassing."

"I should have thought you would have been used to them by now."

"I have not had very many paid me before today," Selina answered.

"Before today?" Lord Howdrith echoed.

"This is really the first party I have been to since I was grown up," Selina told him.

It was true. There had been few parties since her mother died and certainly none like this one.

She thought that Lord Howdrith was looking at her in surprise, and she was thankful when Quintus Tiverton, who had been dancing with Caroline Letessier, came towards them.

"I have a feeling, Selina," he said, "that you are ready to go home."

"I do not wish to drag you away if you are enjoying yourself," Selina replied.

"I have been invited to a gaming-party at a private Villa," Quintus Tiverton said. "So if I take you back to the Hotel first, I shall have done my duty."

Selina felt like saying that she had no wish to drag him away from the party, or prevent him from going straight on to another, but she knew that she could not drive to the Hotel alone.

She rose to her feet.

"Good-night, Lord Howdrith," she said politely.

"I will call at your Hotel tomorrow afternoon," he replied. "Will two o'clock suit you?"

Selina looked at Quintus Tiverton.

"I am sure that Selina will be delighted to accept your invitation," he said. "Good-night, Howdrith."

"Good-night, Tiverton."

Selina said good-night to her host and hostess. Then as they moved towards the door Caroline Letessier ran after them.

"I must see you, Quintus," she said in a low voice, her hand on his arm. "You know where I am staying. Will you come and see me tomorrow?"

"How could I refuse such an invitation?" he asked as he lifted her hand to his lips.

"Good-night, Caroline," he added. "Try not to set all Baden-Baden by the ears. I understand everything was more or less quiet and peaceful until your arrival."

"Then it is time I woke them up," Caroline Letessier said with mischief in her eyes.

Quintus Tiverton laughed, kissed her hand again,

and putting his arm round Selina drew her towards the door.

When the flunkey at the Villa had found them a carriage they drove towards the Hotel Stephanie.

"Madame Letessier is very . . . attractive," Selina said in a small voice.

"She always has been," Quintus Tiverton replied.

"Did you know her in Paris?" Selina asked.

"Many years ago, on my first visit," he answered. "She had an unquenchable verve and was essentially Parisian."

"Is that what you . . . admire?" Selina asked, thinking how Caroline Letessier's dark hair, irregular features, and dancing eyes were in complete contrast to her own looks.

"I have never met anyone who did not admire Caroline," Quintus Tiverton said briefly.

They drove in silence until they reached the Hotel.

"You will be all right?" Quintus Tiverton asked as he saw her through the door into the brilliantly lit Hall.

"Yes, of course," Selina replied. "What time do you think you will be back?"

"Long after you are asleep," he smiled. "Shall we say somewhere about dawn? It is the traditional time for the return of a gambler."

He saw her eyes searching his face and he said quietly:

"Go to bed and do not worry about anything, Selina. You have got off to a splendid start. You were a great success tonight. Everyone admired you."

He saw the colour flush into her face at his compliment.

"Thank you," she answered. "Good-night, Quintus."

It was the first time she had used his Christian name, although, she told herself, as he was pretending to be her brother, she must get used to doing so.

She turned away towards the stairs which would lead her up to her bed-room.

She fell asleep immediately on getting into bed, being extremely tired after the punishment she had received the night before and the long ride. Much later she awoke with a start to hear a door shut in the next room.

She could see a faint light beneath the curtains drawn across her window and knew that Quintus had been right when he had said he would not be back until after dawn.

She had an irresistible impulse to call out to him; to tell him she was awake and ask him if he had made money at the gaming-table.

Then she told herself that it would only annoy him to be questioned and perhaps make him angry that she should be watching his movements, noting the time of his return.

No man liked the feeling of being spied on, and she had a feeling that Quintus Tiverton, of all people, would fight to preserve his independence.

He had never married, and yet there must have been women, many women as beautiful if not more so than Caroline Letessier, in his life.

Lying in the darkness, listening to Quintus moving about the room next door, Selina found herself remembering how he had laughed at Caroline Letessier's jokes; how she had kissed his cheek, and how she had asked him to come to see her tomorrow.

Was that why Quintus Tiverton had been so glad for her to go driving with Lord Howdrith? He certainly would not wish to take her with him to Caroline Letessier's Villa.

Selina felt depressed and apprehensive.

She could see that she was an encumbrance and a bother, and there was no doubt that Quintus Tiverton would wish to be rid of her as quickly as possible, in fact, as soon as he could find her a suitable husband.

Did he visualise Lord Howdrith as being suitable?

She knew nothing about him. He might be married like Sir John Wilton. Besides, was it likely that an English nobleman, one who she was certain was aware of his own consequence, would wish to marry her?

No, Quintus Tiverton would have to find her someone far less important. But were they likely to meet an ordinary man in the Drawing-Rooms of Caroline Letessier or Léonide Leblanc?

There were so many difficulties and problems, so many questions that appeared to be unanswerable, that Selina felt herself frightened of what might lie ahead.

Then she told herself severely that she should be grateful.

If it had not been for Quintus Tiverton she would at this moment be the prisoner of Mrs. Devilin, perhaps having endured another beating at her hands once they had arrived in Baden-Baden.

"I am so lucky, so very, very lucky," she whispered. But somehow there was a little sob behind the words.

The following morning Selina was almost dressed when there came a knock at the communicating door.

"Can I come in?" Quintus Tiverton asked.

"Oh, you are awake?" she exclaimed. "I expected you to be very late rising this morning."

He entered her room wearing riding-breeches.

"I am going to blow away the cob-webs and the atmosphere of wine and cigars by riding for at least an hour," he said. "As a matter of fact I am going up to the race-course."

"Can I come with you?" Selina asked.

Quintus Tiverton hesitated for a moment and then he said:

"I never thought of it, but you can accompany me if it pleases you. You can ride Jim's horse. It is better than that hack we hired from the Inn."

"I am prepared to ride anything on four legs, if I can come with you," Selina said.

"Then hurry!" he commanded. "And when you are ready, I have something to tell you."

One of the garments Quintus Tiverton had bought her, and which fortunately was ready, was a riding-habit. It was very elegant and in the fashion set by the Empress Eugénie, and was made of white piqué.

There was a hat with a small brim to wear with it, the crown encircled by a gauze veil which matched the blue of Selina's eyes.

She knew as soon as she appeared that Quintus Tiverton was pleased with her appearance, and as they set off from the Hotel towards the race-course he said:

"That habit you are wearing was certainly worth the expense."

"I am very thankful you should think so," Selina replied. "I could not have been seen in Baden-Baden in what I was wearing yesterday."

"No, indeed," he smiled, "although perhaps it was more appropriate for the respectable Miss Tiverton than the outfit you are wearing now."

"Must I be respectable?" Selina asked, thinking of the gaiety and piquancy of Caroline Letessier's face, but not meaning it really seriously.

Quintus Tiverton answered her gravely:

"That is the part you have chosen," he said, "and it is most important that people should realise the fact."

"You mean . . ." Selina began.

Then she realised why the Frenchman with whom she had danced last night had looked at her in a manner she had resented, and why she instinctively wished to avoid dancing with him any further.

However, before she could answer, Quintus Tiverton said:

"What I wished to tell you was that I have decided to move from the Stephanie into a Villa which I heard last night was to let. I have sent Jim to look at it this morning, and if it is suitable we shall go there today."

"A Villa?" Selina exclaimed in surprise. "But surely that will be expensive?"

"Very much cheaper than staying at the Stephanie," Quintus Tiverton replied.

She thought he sounded grim, and after a moment she said tentatively:

"We cannot afford it anymore?"

"We could never afford it in the first place," he answered, "but I could hardly expect you to sleep last night by the wayside. This Villa is small and near the fashionable Lindenstrasse, and if we are not invited out for meals we can eat quite simply at home. Jim is used to buying cheaply in a market."

"I think it is a wonderful idea," Selina said excitedly. "Can we go and look at it?"

"We will go after our ride," Quintus Tiverton promised. "First I need exercise."

As soon as they reached some open ground where they could gallop, he set off at a tremendous pace and Selina was glad to find that she could keep up with him.

She knew she rode well, and it was a joy to be aware that she looked very elegant in her white piqué habit, and that her mount, if not superlative horse-flesh, was adequate.

When they had galloped nearly a mile, Quintus Tiverton pulled up his horse and looked at Selina's flushed face and smiling lips.

"That's better!" he said. "If one could only gamble in the open air, I would enjoy it more."

"Did you win last night?" Selina enquired.

She knew that she should not have asked the question; yet it came to her lips before she could prevent it.

"I won a great deal at one time," Quintus Tiverton replied, "and then in the last few hands my host swept away nearly everything that any of us had acquired."

"What is his name?" Selina asked.

"Baron Bernstoff," Quintus Tiverton answered. "He is a German and, I believe, a very rich man. He is also an extremely proficient gambler."

"Better than you?" Selina asked.

"I am not sure," Quintus Tiverton replied. "He suddenly won back from me last night quite a considerable fortune which I had acquired during the first three or four hours after we had started to play.

"To tell you the truth, Selina, I have been wondering ever since what I did wrong. It is not often I am defeated at what I consider my own particular sport."

"Will you play with him again?" Selina asked.

"Most certainly!" Quintus Tiverton answered. "The same guests who were there last night have been invited again."

"Perhaps tonight you will be really successful," Selina said.

"I was successful, damnit!" Quintus Tiverton exclaimed almost irritably. "That is what annoys me. When one has a run of good luck, it is very unusual for it to change at the very last moment, just when we had decided it was time to go home."

"I can see it must be very annoying," Selina sympathised. "At the same time, you are so clever that I am sure you will win tonight, and this time you will keep it."

"You encourage me," Quintus Tiverton said with a smile. "Let us hope you are right."

They rode back to the town and after some little difficulty found the Villa which Quintus Tiverton had heard was to let.

The moment Selina saw it she realised that it was just where she would like to stay.

It was small and encircled by high yew-hedges. In the garden there were cyprus trees and a small fountain, the water jetting out from a dolphin held in the arms of a small, fat Cupid.

Inside, the Villa consisted of little more than four rooms; a Salon and Dining-Room downstairs, and two bed-rooms on the first floor, each with its own bath-room.

It was exquisitely decorated and Selina exclaimed with delight as she went from room to room.

"How could it possibly be to let?" she asked.

"It belongs to a very successful Parisian actress," he replied, "who was here earlier in the Season because she is a great believer in the efficaciousness of the waters. But she has to appear in a new play and so she has returned to Paris, instructing the Agents to let her Villa to whomever they can trust not to make a mess of it."

He smiled and added:

"The money is really immaterial. She is under the protection of the Prince Napoleon."

Selina was still for a moment and then she said:

"Is every woman in Baden-Baden a *cocotte?*"

"You sound disapproving," Quintus Tiverton exclaimed almost aggressively.

"No ... no, of course I am not," Selina replied hastily. "It is just that the men seem so distinguished, while the ladies ..."

She paused.

"Well, finish your sentence," he said in a hard voice.

"They are so ... lovely," Selina faltered. "At the

same time, when there was that . . . argument last night, they suddenly seemed to become . . . well . . . rather common."

"If you want the sanctity of respectable houses, if you want to meet the social élite, you should not have come with me," Quintus Tiverton snapped.

Selina knew he was angry and going towards him she put out her hands a little piteously as she said:

"P-please . . . please . . . you must not think I am criticising. It is just that I am trying to understand a life I did not know existed. I did not know there were women like Madame Letessier and Madame Leblanc. But, as you say, they are so much more amusing, gay, and vivacious than other ladies might be."

Quintus Tiverton ignored her out-stretched hands and walked across the room to the window.

They were standing in the bed-room which Selina knew must have belonged to the actress who owned the house.

It was decorated in pale pink satin and the drapes of the bed fell from a golden corola on which naked Cupids gambolled with each other and doves fluttered above their heads.

The bed-spread was of valuable lace over satin and the Aubusson carpet was a riot of roses and blue ribbon. There were mirrors on every wall reflecting and rereflecting herself in her white dress and Quintus Tiverton's suddenly scowling expression.

"I am sorry . . . please . . . I am sorry if I have said anything wrong," Selina said pleadingly. "You have been so kind; so wonderful to me! You must not think for a moment that I am finding fault or being anything but abjectly and humbly grateful."

"I do not want your gratitude," he said. "I am trying to do what is best for you, but I suppose I know in my heart that it is wrong."

"Why should it be wrong?" Selina asked.

"Because you should not associate with these women. You should never have heard of *cocottes* or *demi-mondaines,* and you should certainly not be introduced to the mistresses who flaunt their lovers as they flaunt their diamonds."

"I . . . I have no . . . alternative," Selina said, "and if it had not been for you . . . you know what would have . . . happened to me."

"I know that, and I suppose it is my only excuse," Quintus Tiverton said. "I only hope to God that things work out as I expect them to do."

"And what do you expect?" Selina asked.

"You know the answer to that," he replied. "Come along, Selina, this house will suit us, and if the ghosts of its previous occupiers haunt us, we have no-one to blame but ourselves!"

He spoke so crossly that Selina could find nothing to say. Instead she followed him down the stairway, wondering how she could have been so stupid as to make him angry.

They drove back to the Hotel in silence to find that Jim had given the order for their clothes to be packed. Their boxes were already downstairs awaiting a carriage to convey them to the Villa.

Selina waited apprehensively while the bill was presented to Quintus Tiverton.

She felt a sudden terror in case he could not meet it, but he drew the appropriate notes from his pocket and she saw in consternation that a great many of them were required.

Then once again they mounted their horses while Jim put their luggage on the box.

As they rode over a bridge crossing the river, Selina said very softly:

"Was it very . . . expensive?"

"If you want the truth, I am practically cleaned out," he answered. "I have to win tonight, or you will have to try again to find that winning number of the Roulette-Wheel."

"Shall I do that?" Selina asked.

"No!" he answered angrily. "I will not have you mixed up in this sort of thing. I will make the money one way or another. All you must do is make yourself pleasant to Lord Howdrith. He is a pompous ass, he always was! But he is rich and unmarried, and he might have a heart he could lose, although I rather doubt it!"

Quintus Tiverton spoke so scathingly that Selina felt herself tremble.

What should she say? What could she do to make things better? It was all her fault that he had spent so much money, and she knew that tonight her gowns would arrive and it would be impossible for him to pay the bill.

Jim however had not only arranged to bring all their luggage to the Villa, he had also found time to buy food for their lunch.

"Can you cook?" Quintus Tiverton asked Selina.

"Of course," she answered, "and I think, without being conceited, I am a good cook!"

"Then you had better take over from Jim," he replied. "He is extremely heavy-handed when it comes to doing anything more complicated than a grilled steak."

Because she felt she could do something other than listen to him being cross with her, Selina having quickly changed from her white piqué riding-habit into a more simple gown ran downstairs to the kitchen.

It was not a very elaborate meal that she prepared, but at least it was beautifully cooked and she knew as he ate an omelette of fine herbs and a Wiener Schnitzel that she had not failed her own estimation of being a good cook.

There was a salad to which she had added a dressing, followed by the famous local cheesecake which Quintus Tiverton had told her she would enjoy.

They sat in the small Dining-Room, which was decorated in Wedgewood blue and ate at a table covered with the finest linen which must itself have cost a fortune.

Quite suddenly Selina laughed.

"What is amusing you?" Quintus Tiverton asked.

His bad temper, she thought, seemed to have evaporated after he had drunk a few glasses of wine and eaten everything she had prepared for him.

"I was just thinking how funny it is," Selina said. "Everything in this Villa is so valuable. You and I are dressed in the latest fashion. We have horses outside; a servant to wait upon us; and the only thing missing is money!"

She laughed again.

"We are in the richest, most luxurious Spa in the world, and really, if we are honest with ourselves, we are paupers!"

"I do not think it is particularly funny," Quintus Tiverton began, and then as he looked at Selina he too laughed.

"You are right," he said. "It is amusing, but you have forgotten two assets we have which are far superior to anything else."

"What are they?" Selina enquired.

"My brains and your beauty," he replied. "I have a feeling that both of these are the winning cards."

Chapter Five

Seated beside Lord Howdrith in his curricle, Selina looked round her.

Baden-Baden was very French in appearance: the style of the houses, the Civic buildings, and the shops all had an elegance not found in German towns.

They drove down the lovely Lichentaler Allee, past the gardens of the Kurhaus, where, Lord Howdrith told Selina, the Duke of Hamilton, for a bet, once led a calf on a blue ribbon.

But while Selina appreciated Lord Howdrith's curricle, his horses, and the expert manner in which he handled them, it was hard to keep her thoughts on anything but Quintus Tiverton.

After they had finished luncheon he had glanced at his gold watch and said:

"Your English admirer will be calling for you in about twenty minutes."

Selina looked at him in surprise and he explained:

"I left a message at the Stephanie, where Lord Howdrith has a suite, to tell him that we have moved here. I understand that he is taking you driving this afternoon."

"I had forgotten," Selina replied. "What are you doing?"

She knew she had hoped that they would be able to do something together, but Quintus Tiverton replied:

"What do you expect a gambler to do but to gamble? I am going back to the tables."

"With the Baron?"

"He has invited the same guests as were there last night. They consisted of three French millionaires, a Russian whose wealth is incalculable, an Austrian whose horses are so outstanding that they will undoubtedly win practically every race next week, and of course myself."

He paused and then said with a laugh that had little humour in it:

"In fact, I am the only professional amongst them and the only person who really needs the money!"

"I am sure you will win this afternoon," Selina said optimistically.

"I have to," Quintus Tiverton replied. "I am still furious with myself for having lost last night all I had gained."

"Was it a very large sum?" Selina enquired.

"It would have saved us from worrying for a few weeks at any rate," Quintus Tiverton answered.

"I wish I could come with you," Selina said with a little sigh.

"Nonsense!" he said sharply. "You know you have to make yourself pleasant to Lord Howdrith and you have to be seen. It is very important for the ladies who wish to proclaim their beauty in Baden-Baden to go driving in the afternoon."

There was a pause, and then Selina said in a small voice:

"Can we dine . . . here . . . tonight?"

As she asked the question she thought of how she could cook Quintus Tiverton some dishes which he would really enjoy. There had not been time to plan anything very elaborate for luncheon.

He seemed to consider her question and then he said:

"We have already had at least half a dozen invitations, including one from Madame Leblanc and another from Madame Letessier."

Selina waited, her eyes on his face.

"Which do you prefer?" he asked.

He looked down at her, their eyes met, and quite suddenly Selina found it impossible to move and hard to breathe.

She felt as if without words they were saying something very close and very intimate to each other.

Then Quintus Tiverton turned away and said sharply:

"We will dine with Madame Letessier. As she and the Grand Duke are new to Baden-Baden, everyone will want to be invited to their Villa. It will enhance your prestige to be one of their first guests."

Selina wanted to argue that she would so much prefer to dine alone with him, but she knew that Quintus Tiverton would not listen. She already had learnt that when he had that steely note in his voice he expected her to obey him.

Besides, had she not given him her word of honour that she would do what he wished?

She walked across the Salon to stand at the window looking out at the small garden.

"Be very charming to Lord Howdrith," he went on. "He might be useful—one never knows."

Selina longed to ask if they could know only people who might be useful now or in the future. Then she told herself that such a question would undoubtedly annoy him.

"Will you be . . . here when I come . . . back?" she asked.

"I shall of course return to change for dinner," he replied. "And I expect that your new gowns will have arrived. It is important that you should be noticed when we arrive at the Casino later in the evening, where we shall undoubtedly go."

"But what about your game with the Baron?" Selina asked.

"I anticipate winning so much this afternoon that I shall be able to attend to you during the evening," he replied, and saw the gladness in her eyes.

"Hurry and get ready, Selina," he added sharply. "Englishmen do not like being kept waiting!"

"That is true," Selina answered. "My father always became furious if Mama and I were late, especially if it made the horses restless."

"With a Frenchman you can be more elusive," Quintus Tiverton said, as if he was following his own train of thoughts.

He paused and Selina waited.

"What were you going to say to me?" she asked after a moment.

"I was going to say that a Frenchman is of little use to you," he answered. "Let us make it quite clear, Selina, since you are ignorant of such matters, that a Frenchman's marriage is always arranged. A French bridegroom expects in return for his name that his bride should bring him a large dowry either in the shape of money or land."

"I would not wish to marry a Frenchman anyway!" Selina said, thinking of the Marquis.

"You will not get the opportunity," Quintus Tiverton went on, "and therefore concentrate on the English or Germans. They are the only races who marry outside their immediate social circles, or would contemplate taking for a wife a woman who has no assets except her beauty."

Selina wondered why it hurt her to listen to Quintus Tiverton talking of her marriage.

'It is not only what he says,' she thought, 'but the way he says it.'

There was something in his voice which made her feel that he was antagonistic to her, and yet she told herself she was being absurd.

He had been so kind, so considerate in thinking of her problems, her future, and she would be extraordinarily ungrateful not to try to please him in every way.

She waited, expecting him to say something else, but he remarked abruptly:

"Go and change, Selina. I have already told you not to keep Lord Howdrith waiting!"

Selina hurried upstairs to the rather garish bed-room where she found that Jim had already unpacked the clothes he had brought from the Stephanie.

There was also an afternoon-dress and hat which must have arrived while they were at luncheon.

It was extremely pretty. The skirt draped in the front to fall in soft folds down the back of the dress, while the tight little bodice accentuated Selina's tiny waist.

It was made of cotton, with pink stripes on a white ground, while the bodice and draping were the colour of the roses blooming outside in the garden.

There was an attractive little hat trimmed with pink rose-buds and Selina knew when she inspected herself in the mirror that she was like a Dresden china figure and she had never looked so attractive.

"I wonder if Quintus will like me in this?" she asked herself.

Picking up her gloves and reticule which matched her gown, she ran downstairs to the Salon.

To her disappointment Quintus Tiverton was not there, and she turned towards the kitchen to find Jim and ask where he was.

"The Master has left, Miss," Jim told her. "I fetched a hired carriage for him as soon as you went upstairs."

"He did not say good-bye to me," Selina said in a forlorn little voice.

"I expect, Miss, he was in a hurry to get his hands on the cards," Jim said, "and it's important he should do. After all, our pockets are empty and we've not yet put down the deposit on the house."

Jim said "we" as if he were part of the family, and Selina knew that he identified himself so closely with Quintus Tiverton's interests that that was in fact exactly what he was.

"It is 'us' against the world," she told herself. "Quintus, Jim, and I, and somehow we must win through."

The question came to her mind as to what would happen when their plans for her marriage had materialised and she would have to leave the other two and go away with this strange husband whom Quintus Tiverton was determined to find for her.

She felt that there was something cold and frightened inside her at the thought, and then she told herself that it had not yet happened and there was no point in being upset until it had.

Perhaps no one would ever offer for her, and then she could remain as Quintus Tiverton's sister as long as he could pay for her.

"Please, God, let him win," she prayed, and heard a carriage drive up to the front door.

There was no doubt that Lord Howdrith had arrived in style. His curricle, in black with yellow wheels which were emblazoned with his crest, was as smart as the two horses which pulled it.

Selina was aware that they were of the highest quality and their silver accoutrements were as smart as the uniform of the groom who sat behind them on a small seat, his cockaded top-hat polished until it shone.

As Lord Howdrith brought his horses to a stand-still, Selina opened the Villa door and stood on the steps.

She saw the admiration in his eyes as he swept his hat from his head, and as the groom helped her in beside him he said:

"You are the most punctual woman I have ever taken out."

"My brother told me that you would be angry if I kept you waiting," Selina replied.

"Do you really anticipate that I could ever be angry with you?" he asked.

There was an intimate note in his voice which surprised her. Last night he had seemed so aloof, almost as if he had forced himself to be pleasant. Now he smiled at her in a familiar manner and started his horses down the narrow drive.

"Will we be safe if we drive in the forest?" Selina asked a little nervously.

She had no desire to encounter bandits without Quintus Tiverton being there to protect her.

"We are not going far from town," Lord Howdrith answered. "My groom and I both are armed and I promise you, Miss Tiverton, that you can trust me to take care of you."

The roads he chose to drive along were very attractive with shady trees and gardens and Villas on either side of them.

But Selina's mind kept wandering away as she wondered how Quintus Tiverton was faring with the Baron.

How wonderful it would be if he came home having won enough money for them to have no worries for at least a week or so!

Then perhaps he could spend more time with her and perhaps sometimes they could be alone.

It was a joy to think that in the Villa they would be able to breakfast together, but it would be even more exciting to cook his luncheon or dinner.

Selina even began to plan in her mind the different

dishes she would concoct and the meat, fish, and game she would ask Jim to buy in the market.

She was so glad that her mother had insisted on her learning to cook and that her father had been extremely fastidious as to what he ate.

Because Quintus Tiverton had lived in Paris he would like French dishes, she thought, and it would be easy to get the cream and butter and truffles and herbs which are essential for French cuisine.

Lord Howdrith made her start when he said unexpectedly:

"You are very silent, Miss Tiverton."

"I was enjoying the drive," Selina said quickly.

"That is what I hoped you would say," he answered, "and perhaps add that you like driving with me?"

"I do," Selina answered. "I think you are very expert with the reins. I am sure when you are riding you have very good hands. My father always said that that was the essential of any good rider."

"You are saying all the things I want to hear," Lord Howdrith smiled. "Shall I respond by telling you how beautiful you are? I thought last night that you were one of the loveliest women I had ever seen. Today I will qualify that opinion by saying you are the loveliest."

Selina looked at him in surprise and then she answered:

"You are very . . . kind, but I always . . . understood that Englishmen seldom pay . . . compliments."

"I am not being complimentary," Lord Howdrith said. "I am merely stating a fact."

Selina looked ahead and wondered what she should reply to that. She had not expected to have this sort of conversation with Lord Howdrith, and she thought how shy it made her and how inexperienced she was.

Madame Letessier would know exactly what to answer if any gentleman said the same sort of thing to her.

She would undoubtedly be witty and amusing, and would accept such a bouquet of words with an elegance that was characteristic of everything she did.

'No wonder Quintus admires her so much,' Selina thought, 'while I am behaving like a silly school-girl!'

Lord Howdrith's next remark was somehow consoling.

"You are so unspoilt, Selina," he said. "That is what I find so fascinating about you."

Selina's eyes widened at the way he addressed her. It was, she well knew, very forward of him to use her Christian name on such a very short acquaintance.

In fact, she knew that her mother would have been astonished if any of their acquaintances had spoken to her in such a manner.

Christian names were used only when people had known each other for a long time and then only in private.

Selina had been quite surprised to hear Léonide Leblanc address the Duc d'Aumale as Henri, after their encounter with the bandits, while later in the evening she had referred to him most punctiliously as "Monsieur le Duc" or "Your Royal Highness."

Caroline Letessier had said "Your Imperial Highness" in almost every sentence when she addressed the Grand Duke.

As if he guessed her thoughts Lord Howdrith said after a moment:

"I see you are surprised that I called you Selina. I know in fact that we have actually only just met, but I feel that I have known you for a long time, and what is more, Selina, I wish to know you very much better."

Selina glanced at him and then looked away again.

"Perhaps I should have waited before I said this," Lord Howdrith said, "but I could see last night that practically every man in the room was ready to make some sort of proposition to you. Though the English are supposed to be slow in making up their minds, I can assure you that I have already made up mine."

Selina grasped her fingers together in her lap.

'What is he trying to say?' she wondered.

Surely he could not be going to ask her to marry him? It was not possible on such a short acquaintance, and besides she was quite convinced that he would not think her grand enough to be his wife.

"Think about me, Selina," Lord Howdrith said, "and we will talk more about ourselves this evening."

While he had been speaking he had lowered his voice because, Selina knew, he was afraid that the groom sitting beside him could overhear their conversation.

It was unlikely, and yet the servant was there and his very presence was restrictive.

They drove for some minutes in silence and Selina realised that they had turned back towards the town.

"Where are you dining tonight?" Lord Howdrith asked.

"With Madame Letessier," Selina replied.

As she spoke she remembered how warmly Caroline Letessier had greeted Quintus Tiverton, and she wished that, instead of going to the Grand Duke's Villa, they were dining with Madame Leblanc.

Quintus Tiverton and Sir John had praised Caroline Letessier's beauty, wit, and charm.

Selina was certain that in the older woman's presence she would be tongue-tied and stupid. Then she told herself that if Lord Howdrith found her attractive, perhaps Quintus Tiverton felt the same.

"I have also been invited," Lord Howdrith was saying, "by the Grand Duke. I knew him when I was in Russia. He is a very intelligent man."

He laughed before he continued:

"It must seem strange to you, as it does to me, how these world-famous notabilities relax when they come to Baden-Baden."

"I suppose His Imperial Highness is of great importance in Russia?" Selina said, for something to say, and was relieved that Lord Howdrith was no longer talking so intimately about herself.

"He is, indeed," Lord Howdrith replied, "and his affection for Caroline Letessier caused a great scandal. The Tsar was not at all pleased."

"So the Grand Duke said last night," Selina remarked.

"At one Ball where I was present," Lord Howdrith said, "Madame Letessier's gown was torn in a waltz. His Imperial Highness repaired the damage by tying the pieces together with his Grand Cordon of the Order of St. Andrew!"

Selina smiled.

"It must have looked very strange."

"She carried it off magnificently," Lord Howdrith enthused. "But then she is a very exceptional person."

'That is what Quintus thinks,' Selina thought, and wished once again that they were not dining that evening with the Grand Duke.

When they reached the Villa and Lord Howdrith drew his horses to a stand-still he took one hand from the reins to lift Selina's fingers to his lips.

"Need I tell you how much I have enjoyed being with you this afternoon?" he asked.

"It was very kind of you to take me driving," Selina replied formally.

"It is something we must do together very, very often," Lord Howdrith said. "As you are as interested in horses as I am, it is yet another subject in which we have a common interest."

Selina took her hand away from his.

"Thank you so much, My Lord," she said in a rather frightened little voice.

She then stood on the steps and watched him drive away, raising his hat as he did so, the gesture being copied by his servant.

"He is quite different from what I expected," she told herself, and went into the Villa.

She had a long time to wait before Quintus Tiverton returned, and she found it impossible to settle to anything.

She tried to read the newspaper but the words seemed to jumble themselves in front of her eyes. She could only listen for the carriage that would bring him back.

She went upstairs to her own bed-room and put ready the things that she would wear that evening.

She did not begin to change because she wanted to talk to him on his return and she knew that it was unlikely that he would come to her bed-room if she had already started to undress.

Three gowns had been delivered while she was out.

They all were extremely attractive, but Selina knew with a sinking of her heart that they were also extremely expensive.

She chose one of pale blue which made her think of the colour of the sky as she and Quintus Tiverton had ridden away together from the Inn.

Selina felt that she would never be able to forget the joy of being able to escape from Mrs. Devilin and knew that Quintus Tiverton would protect her.

"How could I have been so fortunate in his being in the next-door attic just when I needed him most?" she asked herself. "If the Inn had not been full, he would never have heard me scream and would never have rescued me."

As she heard the carriage draw up outside the front door she ran eagerly through the small corridor to await Quintus Tiverton on the steps while he was still paying the driver.

Then as he turned round and she saw the expression on his face she knew without words that he had not won, as she had prayed he might do.

He walked past her into the Salon and Selina, having followed him, waited just inside the door.

"I know what you are longing to ask me," he said harshly. "The answer is that what happened last night happened again this afternoon."

"You lost?"

"I lost what I had gained," he said, "practically all of it."

"You had won a lot?"

"A great deal, and so had another man at the table. Then in the last three hands our host had phenomenal luck. I can hardly believe it possible."

The way he said it made Selina ask:

"You think that the game was not quite ... straight?"

"I am almost sure it was not," Quintus Tiverton replied. "But I was on my guard, Selina, and although I watched every move he made, every card he handled, there was nothing I could see that was not completely and absolutely above-board."

"Could it really be chance that he won at the very last minute, as he did last night?" Selina enquired.

"That is what I keep asking myself, but I cannot find the answer."

"Have you ... any money ... left?" Selina enquired hesitatingly.

"A little," he replied, "because instinctively I anticipated that this might happen. I drew back, but not before I had lost what to me was a fortune on a seemingly unbeaten hand. I still have enough to challenge the Baron again tonight, and that is what I intend to do."

Selina gave a little cry.

"Are you wise? Suppose he wins again, and then you are left with nothing?"

Quintus Tiverton walked across the small Salon and back again.

"I am absolutely convinced," he said, "that there is something strange about this. The others just accepted that it was the luck of the draw, but I am not so sure. I cannot help feeling that there is something uncanny, or crooked, about the Baron's good fortune."

"What could he do that you would not notice?" Selina asked.

"That is exactly what I have been asking myself," Quintus Tiverton replied. "There was no mirror behind me, no possibility of his palming the cards. New sealed packs were opened before each fresh deal. I have not a single clue that there is anything wrong, except my instinct."

"I have always believed that one should trust one's instinct," Selina said. "How I wish I could come with you tonight! I have a feeling that just as I knew what numbers would turn up at Roulette, I might be able to sense what the Baron was doing."

"Unfortunately that is impossible," Quintus Tiverton replied.

Then he stood still in the centre of the room.

"But why should it be?" he asked. "Why should you not come with me? You would not be particularly welcome in an all-male party; but if it annoys the Baron, what does it matter? If I lose tonight I shall certainly not be able to play with him again."

"You mean you will take me?" Selina asked breathlessly.

"I shall have to think of an excuse," Quintus Tiverton said, "for not leaving you at the Casino with our dinner hostess when I join the Baron at his Villa."

He gave a sudden exclamation.

"I have it!"

Selina watched him, her eyes on his face.

"We will not dine with the Grand Duke," he said, "we will dine here. Afterwards we will go to the Baron's Villa and I will explain that you were frightened at being left alone in an empty house."

"Could you do that?" Selina asked.

"It is what I have every intention of doing," Quintus Tiverton replied. "That is the solution, Selina. I only hope you will be perceptive enough to find out what I have missed. I am absolutely convinced that I am either extremely obtuse, or the Baron is a magician."

"I am sure I can help you," Selina cried, "and I am glad, so very, very glad that we can dine here together."

They dined late because Jim not only had to take a note of apology to Madame Letessier, he also had to buy the ingredients which Selina needed for Quintus Tiverton's dinner.

As she had so little time she did not make the mistake of trying anything too complicated. Instead she gave him a simple menu and one which he pronounced delicious.

"I thought you said you had no talents," he said with a smile as Jim removed the plates from the last course.

"They are not ones which are very marketable," Selina answered. "I do not think anyone would wish to employ me as their cook."

"They might wish to do so," Quintus Tiverton replied, "but I have a feeling that the rest of their staff would object! Too many of the guests would feel obliged to visit you in the kitchen, and that would certainly upset the protocol of the servants'-hall."

Selina laughed.

"I am sure you are right, but fortunately Jim is only too delighted not to have to cook for you. He told me you were very critical."

"I am certainly not criticising anything you have cooked for me so far," Quintus Tiverton replied. "In fact I can only compliment you and hope that this high standard of cuisine will continue."

"If I had had more time, you would have had an even better meal," Selina said. "If you will dine here tomorrow night, I promise you a feast fit for Lucullus."

"It depends, of course, on whether we can afford to eat at all," Quintus Tiverton replied.

Selina remembered his words when she went upstairs after dinner to collect a wrap to wear over her blue gown.

When she had been cooking she had covered it with a large apron. The heat from the stove had brought the colour to her cheeks and loosened some little curls round her forehead.

She looked very young and lovely as she came down the stairs to where Quintus Tiverton was waiting for her in the Hall.

"I should have taken you to the Casino, where you would have caused a sensation," he said, "rather than to a dull party where a lot of men will have eyes only for the piles of gold in front of them on the table."

"I am happy as long as I can be with you," Selina answered.

Once again their eyes met, and they looked at each other before Quintus Tiverton turned away abruptly.

"Come along," he said. "I can only hope, for your sake, that the evening will not be too long drawn out."

"We do not expect anything to happen until the last twenty minutes of play?" Selina queried as they got into the hired carriage which was waiting for them outside.

"That is what I anticipate," Quintus Tiverton said. "It seems to me as if the Baron waits until one or two of his guests have won a fortune and then he challenges them. This afternoon it was myself and the same Frenchman who lost last night."

He gave a sigh.

"Perhaps I am wrong, Selina, but I am very experienced in these affairs, and I suppose all gamblers rely to an enormous extent on their intuition. Mine now tells me there is something wrong."

"Then I must find out what it is," Selina said in a low voice.

"You are very understanding," Quintus Tiverton remarked. "Most women would be angry and resentful at not going to the parties that are being given tonight, and not appearing in all their glory at the Casino."

"You know I would much rather be with you," Selina said simply.

"Which is not what you should prefer!" he replied. "You have to be seen; to be admired; to command attention. You know that as well as I do."

"I know, if I am truthful, that I do not want any of those things," Selina answered. "Compliments make me feel uncomfortable, and I really have no wish to be the centre of attention."

"Then you are very different from the majority of your sex," Quintus Tiverton said dryly.

Selina did not answer, and she wondered if he thought she was being ungrateful after all the money he had spent on her.

Then she told herself that he had asked her to tell the truth, and the truth was that she had never enjoyed a dinner more than the one they had just had together.

To see his handsome face across the table; to know that he was talking to her and was not being distracted by other women, was a delight beyond words.

They were nearly at the Baron's Villa and as they turned in at the gate Selina slipped her hand into Quintus Tiverton's.

"I shall be praying that I can help you," she said. "I am sure I shall be lucky for you. I am certain of it!"

He raised her fingers to his lips and as she felt his mouth against her skin she felt a little quiver of delight run through her and found herself wondering what it would feel like if Quintus Tiverton kissed her lips.

At the thought a thrill swept through her body, and then she told herself that she was being ridiculous.

Was it likely that he would wish to kiss her, when

Madame Letessier looked at him with invitation in her
eyes and was bold enough to kiss his cheek in front of
everyone else?

The Baron's Villa was very impressive. There were
at least half a dozen footmen in resplendent livery to
assist them from the carriage and take Selina's wrap
and Quintus Tiverton's hat and cape.

They were escorted pompously across the Hall by a
butler who flung open two large mahogany doors to an-
nounce:

"Miss Selina Tiverton, and Mr. Quintus Tiverton,
Herr Baron!"

Selina saw the look of surprise on the Baron's face as
he moved towards them and Quintus Tiverton explained quickly:

"You must forgive me, Baron, for bringing my sister
with me, but we have today moved into a new Villa
and have not yet had time to engage many servants.
My sister was afraid of being left alone, and I felt sure
you would understand."

"I am honoured by Miss Tiverton's presence," the
Baron replied in a guttural voice. "At the same time, I
am afraid she will find it extremely dull."

"I am quite happy to read a book or the newspa-
pers," Selina answered. "I do not wish to be a
nuisance."

"You could never be that," the Baron replied gal-
lantly. "At the same time, I wish there was some way
that I could entertain you."

"I am quite content just to be here with my brother,"
Selina answered. "I can only apologise for being such a
coward that I would not stay alone in the Villa without
him."

"It all comes of playing chaperon to my sister in
Baden-Baden instead of taking her, as I should have
done, back to England," Quintus Tiverton said lightly.

Selina looked at the Baron and saw that he was a
middle-aged, thick-set man with characteristic Ger-
manic features and coarse grey hair cropped closely in
a manner which she thought extremely unbecoming.

He was not an attractive man by any means. He had

a heavy moustache, wore spectacles, and was, she thought, almost aggressively authoritative.

The Frenchmen in the party immediately paid her extravagant compliments and while she was blushing a little at their flattery the Baron said briskly:

"Now that we all are here, let us get to work. I feel sure, as Miss Tiverton is waiting for her brother to take her home, that it will be best for us not to be as late as we were last night."

"I have no wish to stay so long," one of the Baron's guests replied. "I have to be up early in the morning to see my horses at the gallop. I have every hope that one of them will wrench the 'Gold Whip' from the Englishman, Lord Howdrith, who is absolutely certain that he will leave Baden-Baden with it in his possession."

It was then that Selina remembered that Lord Howdrith would be waiting for her at Madame Letessier's.

Would he wonder what had happened? Might he think she had deliberately refused the invitation because she did not wish to meet him again?

Either way, Selina told herself, it was of little consequence. What really mattered was that she should watch the card-players to see what the Baron did to make himself so successful a gamester.

The table was set up in the centre of the room. There was a chandelier with bright gas globes immediately over it, and it was absolutely impossible in that position for any of the players to gain any advantage from their immediate surroundings.

Selina, who had seated herself at the fireside with a newspaper in her hand, which she had no intention of reading, saw that the packs of cards which had been placed on a small table beside the Baron were all wrapped in white paper and sealed.

She could not help drawing in her breath a little apprehensively as she saw the very large amount of gold coins that every player had in front of him.

She noticed too that Quintus Tiverton's pile was rather smaller than the others.

Even so, she was quite certain that it was everything he possessed.

The Baron dealt and the players placed their bets.

He offered cards to those who wished to draw, and as they started to bid against each other, Selina, listening, heard the different tones of their voices.

Quintus's voice was entirely expressionless, but the Frenchmen could not suppress a little eager lilt when they were winning and sometimes a hesitant note when they were not sure that their cards were good enough.

Selina also noticed as the evening went on that some of the players betrayed themselves by small mannerisms.

Sometimes they tapped their fingers on the table in moments of indecision; one man's eye-lids flickered when he had a good hand; another swallowed a little convulsively; a third had a muscle which twitched at the side of his cheek.

Only the Baron seemed to have no mannerisms, and Quintus was deliberately self-effacing so that anyone watching him would gain no information from anything he said or did.

An hour passed and then another. In between the deals, servants brought drinks and sandwiches which they offered to the players.

As the third hour started Selina saw that Quintus Tiverton had a huge pile of gold coins in front of him.

She rose as the Baron was dealing and went from the room. Finding several footmen in the Hall, she asked the way to a bed-chamber.

A flunkey led the way upstairs and opened, off a square landing, the door of a very ornate and impressive bed-room.

The curtains were over-tasselled and over-rich; the furniture, heavy mahogany of the type a German would find both luxurious and substantial.

Opening off of the bed-room was a bath-room which, Selina found, contained three doors. There was one onto the landing, one communicating with the bed-room into which she had been shown, and there was another on the opposite wall.

She washed her hands and then very gently opened the third door.

As she had expected, it led into another bed-room, and this she saw at a glance was the Baron's room, unless it was occupied by someone who was staying with him.

The gas-lights were lowered but it was easy to see a huge, ugly mahogany bed, a dressing table with a circular mirror attached, while a large carved wardrobe seemed to occupy almost one wall.

The door onto the landing was closed, and Selina moved across the room.

She told herself that if anyone came and discovered her she would say that she was looking for a comb or a brush with which to tidy her hair.

She looked at the dressing-table and saw that she was right in thinking that she was in the Baron's room, because his silver brushes were engraved with the Coat-of-Arms she had noticed on the buttons of his servants' livery.

There were two hair-brushes, two clothes-brushes, and several silver-topped bottles; all with the same engraving. There was also a leather case containing his razors and a stud-box, besides a button-hook, shoe-lift, and a number of bottles, some containing pills.

It was all meticulously neat and Selina thought with a smile that the Baron obviously had a very orderly mind.

Also on the dressing-table were two pairs of spectacles.

'He is making quite certain that he has a pair in reserve,' Selina thought to herself. 'Perhaps without spectacles his eyesight is so poor he cannot see the cards.'

She looked at herself in the large mirror as she spoke, saw her own reflection, and knew that she was looking very attractive.

'How lucky I am to have good eyesight,' she thought. 'What could be more disastrous for a woman than to have to wear glasses?'

She remembered that Quintus Tiverton had said that Madame Letessier carried lorgnettes.

"When I am old," Selina told herself, "I shall carry them too. They are much more attractive than spectacles."

As she thought of it she picked up a pair of the

Baron's and placed them on her small nose. They were
certainly extremely unbecoming!

But when she looked through them at her own reflection she realised that the Baron's eyesight must need
very little adjustment.

The fact that she was wearing them made no difference to her vision.

'Perhaps they are only for reading,' she thought.

Then she looked towards the pill-bottles, wondering
if the small print on the label would appear larger or
clearer.

As she did so, she saw that lying beside the bottles
was a paint-brush. It was a very slim, pointed one and
she wondered what use the Baron had for it.

He did not seem the type of man who would wish to
paint a picture! But she remembered that her mother
had sometimes used a paint-brush to darken her eye-
brows slightly before she went anywhere important.

"I think a face looks expressionless without eye-
brows," she had told Selina with a little laugh. "But do
not tell your father I am so vain as to touch mine up.
He does not approve of any aids to beauty."

The Baron could hardly wish to touch up his eye-
brows, Selina thought. Then she noticed that there was
a slightly luminous tip to the brush.

It puzzled her what it would be used for. Then she
perceived that a small bottle beside those containing
pills gleamed in exactly the same way.

She pulled off the spectacles to look at it more
closely and she realised, as they left her nose, that neither the brush nor the bottle showed any colour except
a natural brown.

Puzzled, she held the spectacles on to her nose again
and knew that she had discovered something important.

Quickly she opened the drawers of the dressing-table. The top one contained handkerchiefs, the one below it, ties; but in the bottom drawer there were stacks
of cards.

Most of them were in their sealed covers, but two
packs were held only with elastic bands. Beside them
was another brush and a small pot of glue.

Selina inspected the cards, first without the glasses,

and then with them on her nose. In the centre of some cards there was a tiny luminous dot.

She turned them over—the court-cards were marked.

Swiftly she put the cards back in the drawer and closed it. Picking up the spectacles, she ran back across the bed-room into the bath-room.

She closed the communicating door, hid the spectacles in her reticule which matched the blue satin of her gown, and a few seconds later she went demurely down the stairs and back into the Salon.

The players did not turn their heads at her entrance and she sat down in the chair where she had been before and took up the newspaper.

She glanced at the clock. It was getting on towards one in the morning.

A quarter of an hour later, as a hand came to an end and the drinks and sandwiches were passed round, the Baron said:

"I think we should have three more deals, and then allow Tiverton to take his sister home. I feel that such a charming and beautiful lady must be very bored."

Selina rose and walked towards the table.

"I have been interested in watching you," she replied, "and it was so kind of you to allow me to stay."

"It has been a pleasure," the Baron said with an attempt at gallantry as he sipped his wine.

Then taking off his spectacles he polished them with his large white handkerchief.

He went on talking as he did so, and Selina, watching him closely, realised that as he finished polishing his spectacles he slipped them into his pocket.

A moment later he brought a pair out again and she was quite certain that they were not the original pair he had been wearing.

She turned to Quintus Tiverton.

"You are looking tired, Quintus," she said in a low voice, which was quite audible to the players on either side of him. "You know if you play cards for a long time without wearing your reading-glasses it gives you a headache. Do put them on, otherwise I know you will be cross in the morning."

As she spoke, she pretended to take from his pocket

the spectacles she had in her reticule and, as she did so, she touched his arm as if to warn him not to protest.

He was however far too quick-witted not to understand that she had a reason for what she was doing.

"You nag me worse than any wife!" he said in a good-humoured voice, and taking the spectacles from her put them on his nose.

The Baron, who had been talking to the gentleman near him at the other end of the table, opened a new pack of cards and asked:

"Are we all ready?"

Selina went back to the chair in which she had been sitting all the evening.

She thought it unwise to draw nearer to the table, but she was sure with a rising sense of excitement that Quintus, by this time, would have noticed the tiny luminous spots on the cards which every player was holding high against his chest, so that they could not be overlooked by their neighbours.

After a moment he put his own cards on the table, and kept his hand over them.

Now the Baron was beginning to increase his wagers by what seemed to Selina almost astronomical amounts.

One by one the other players fell out until only Quintus and the Baron were left

Then as the betting grew higher and higher she heard a note of anger in the Baron's voice as he laid down his cards and Quintus had won.

Two more hands were played and each time Quintus was the winner.

"I cannot understand it," the Baron said harshly, "my luck seems to have deserted me!"

There was no doubt that he was extremely put out as he rose to push back his chair with a disdainful gesture.

"You must not grudge Tiverton his revenge," one of the Frenchmen remarked. "After all, he was a big loser last night and this afternoon."

It was obviously with an effort that the Baron replied grudgingly:

"No, no, of course not! Do we play again tomorrow?"

Quintus Tiverton was collecting his gains. After he

filled his handkerchief and knotted it together Selina said:

"Perhaps some of the coins will go in my bag."

He filled her reticule and his pockets, and there were still some left for him to carry in his hand.

"A delightful evening, Baron," he said. "I cannot tell you how much I have enjoyed myself."

"You will be coming tomorrow?" the Baron asked. It was more a statement than a question.

"I am not certain," Quintus replied. "I feel I have neglected my poor little sister quite abominably, and must make up for it by escorting her to some of the many amusing parties to which we have both been invited."

"If you cannot come in the afternoon, I shall expect you in the evening."

There was no mistaking the note of authority in the Baron's voice, as if he commanded Quintus Tiverton to obey him.

"Do not wait for me if I do not turn up," Quintus Tiverton replied. "As I have already said, it entirely depends on my sister."

"I can think of no better reason for refusing to gamble," one of the Frenchmen said. "Let us all play truant and escort the delectable Miss Tiverton!"

"I shall expect you here!" the Baron said with a sharp edge to his voice.

They said their farewells to the other gamblers, and only as they drove away from the Villa did Quintus Tiverton put his arms round Selina and hug her.

"You wonderful, wonderful girl!" he exclaimed. "How did you find out? How did you know that that was what he had been doing?"

There was a note of elation in his voice as he pulled Selina close against his chest and hugged her.

At his touch, at the feel of his arms, at the sight of his face so near to hers, she knew that she loved him!

Chapter Six

When they arrived at the Villa, Quintus Tiverton carried the money into the Salon and pushing aside some china ornaments set the coins down on a small round table.

Selina looked with delight as he arranged the piles until they practically covered the table.

"How much have you won?" she asked breathlessly.

"Very nearly a thousand pounds in English money," he replied. "That at least will keep the wolf from the door for a short while."

"We can pay our debts?" Selina asked.

"We will do that tomorrow," he agreed.

Then he sat back in his chair and said:

"Tell me exactly what happened."

Selina related how she had gone upstairs and entered the Baron's bed-room.

"I did not know what I was looking for," she said, "and yet vaguely I felt I might find something which would be a clue to what you suspected."

She went on to explain how she had picked up the spectacles and placed them on her nose to see how she looked.

She did not add that she had been determined when she was old to carry a lorgnette like Madame Letessier did.

"Then what happened?" Quintus Tiverton enquired.

"I saw a small paint-brush," Selina answered, "and could not imagine why the Baron should need one."

"No-one would suspect him of being artistic," Quintus Tiverton agreed.

"And I noticed the luminous tip."

Selina went on to explain how she had found the bottle on the dressing-table, the cards in the bottom of

113

a drawer, and with them another paint-brush and a pot of glue.

"What I cannot understand," she said, "is why the Baron, who is obviously very rich, should stoop to obtaining money by cheating."

"He is rich, that is true," Quintus Tiverton agreed, "but there are men, however wealthy they may be, who cannot bear to lose money."

He paused for a moment as if he was thinking and then he said:

"I am convinced that the Baron played the game entirely straight until the last few hands. I imagine too that had he won a great deal of money, he would not have changed his spectacles."

"I wonder if he wears spectacles at other times?" Selina asked.

"I have seen him with a monocle when he is not sitting at a card-table," Quintus Tiverton replied, "but for many men that is entirely an affectation. As you say, there appeared to be no magnification in the lenses of his spectacles. I imagine he does not really require any aids to his eyesight."

"What are you going to do?" Selina enquired.

"Nothing!" Quintus Tiverton replied.

"Perhaps when he finds that a pair of his spectacles are missing, he will realise what has happened."

"Yes, I think that is likely," Quintus Tiverton agreed, "in which case he will not press me as he was doing this evening to accept his hospitality."

"He cannot hurt you?" Selina asked.

Quintus Tiverton shook his head.

"There is nothing he can do to me without exposing himself," he said. "After all, the mere suspicion that the game might be rigged would deter even the most ardent of gamblers from accepting the Baron's invitation."

"All the same, he will be your enemy," Selina said, "and I am afraid."

Quintus Tiverton smiled at the fear in her voice.

"I promise you, Selina, I will look after myself."

"I dislike the Baron," she said in a low voice, "and we are in a . . . foreign country."

As she spoke she had a terrifying thought that the Baron might insist on a duel or, worse still, hire men to assault Quintus Tiverton perhaps on a dark night when he was coming back from the Casino.

She had heard of such things happening and she was quite certain, having seen the Baron, that he was quite capable of resorting to such measures if it suited his purpose.

"You are not to worry about me," Quintus Tiverton said.

As he spoke he put out his hand and laid it on Selina's.

He felt her quiver and there was a look of enquiry in his eyes.

She turned her face to his and for a moment neither of them could move. Then as they looked at each other there was the sound of a carriage drawing up outside the door.

Selina sprang to her feet.

"It might be the Baron," she said in a whisper.

Quintus Tiverton rose too and opening a drawer of the *secretaire* he started to transfer the gold coins from the table to the drawer.

They heard the front-door-bell ring in the kitchen, and as Jim's footsteps moved slowly across the marble Hall the last coin was in the drawer, and Quintus Tiverton shut it and turned the key.

There was the sound of a man's voice before Jim opened the door of the Salon and said:

"Lord Howdrith to see you, Sir."

Selina felt herself relax and there was a feeling of relief as she echoed in surprise:

"Lord Howdrith?"

He came into the room looking exceedingly smart in his evening-clothes.

"Forgive me," he said, "for calling at such a late hour, but as I passed the Villa I saw your lights, so I knew you were awake."

"We have only just returned," Quintus Tiverton said. "Do come in, Howdrith, and sit down. Would you like a glass of wine?"

"Thank you, no," Lord Howdrith replied, "I en-

joyed a very sumptuous and exotic dinner with the
Grand Duke. I expected to find you both there."

Selina looked at Quintus Tiverton.

"When I went driving with His Lordship this afternoon, I thought that was where we would be dining,"
she explained.

"We had to change our plans," Quintus Tiverton
said, "but I am sure there were far too many other
guests for you to have missed us in particular."

"I missed your sister," Lord Howdrith replied.

He settled himself on the sofa covered in blue bro-
cade.

"You are quite certain there is nothing I can offer
you?" Quintus Tiverton asked.

"Nothing," Lord Howdrith replied firmly, "but I
would like a private word with you, if it is possible."

"Then I will retire to bed," Selina said. "Thank you
again, My Lord, for our most enjoyable drive."

She curtseyed as Lord Howdrith rose to his feet,
saying:

"Tomorrow I plan to take you for a drive round the
Margrave's Castle. It is very impressive."

"I am not quite certain what our plans are," Selina
said quickly.

She was hoping that, now that there was no urgency
for Quintus Tiverton to play cards in the afternoon, she
could be with him.

"We will make our plans at breakfast," Quintus
Tiverton said as if he realised what she was thinking.
"Sleep well, Selina, and thank you once again."

She knew why he was thanking her and she gave
him a lovely little smile over her shoulder as she turned
towards the door.

Lord Howdrith opened it for her and once again she
said good-night before she crossed the Hall and pro-
ceeded up the staircase towards her bed-room.

It was annoying, she thought, that Lord Howdrith
should have arrived just when she and Quintus Tiverton were alone.

When he had touched her hand she had felt a sensation so exciting and so unlike anything she had ever felt
before that she had known, even as she knew when his

arms went round her in the carriage, that she loved him overwhelmingly.

She must have loved him, she supposed, ever since the moment he had come into the attic where she was crying, looking so handsome, so smart, that he had seemed like a creature from another world come to rescue her from the very depths of despair.

Then he had taken her away with him, and every moment they had been together had been a rapture and a joy because, although she had not realised it, she was already in love.

"I love him!" she told herself as she crossed her bed-room floor to stand staring into a mirror at the far end of the room.

In her blue gown and with the gas-light shining on her fair hair she knew that she looked very attractive.

"I love him!" she repeated, "but it is impossible for him ever to love me."

She felt humbly that she had so little to offer him. She was not witty, amusing, or talented. She did not know how to flirt or look provocatively fascinating as did the other women whom he admired. Worst of all, she had no money!

With a little throb of anguish she remembered how expensive she had been already.

"I am nothing but an expensive encumbrance," she told herself severely, and wished as she had never wished before in her life that she had wealth, position, perhaps a house and lands that she could offer the man she loved.

"That is what Quintus should have," she told herself, "an Estate, a house that is worthy of him, and a stable filled with fine horses."

She was sure that if all those things were his he would no longer be interested in gambling, and perhaps not even in lovely women like Caroline Letessier.

The mere thought of them was like a dagger piercing her heart. She turned away from the mirror impatiently because she felt that the reflection she saw there was not enough; not nearly enough to gain the man she loved.

Downstairs, following Selina's departure, there was a silence, and then Quintus Tiverton asked:

"Why did you want to see me?"

"I want to talk to you about Selina," Lord Howdrith replied.

"I am listening," Quintus Tiverton said a trifle grimly.

"Just before I left England," Lord Howdrith went on, "I was journeying to Dover preparatory to embarking for the crossing to Calais, and I stayed on the way with a cousin of mine who lives in Canterbury in Kent. They have a fifteen-year-old daughter who had a friend staying with her. Her name was Annette Tiverton!"

There was silence for a moment and then Quintus Tiverton said:

"Selina is not my mistress. Owing to circumstances which are unnecessary for me to relate, I was more or less forced into the position of being her guardian. The simplest way to explain our relationship was to introduce her as my sister."

"It is just unfortunate that I should have actually met your real sister," Lord Howdrith said.

"Let me repeat," Quintus Tiverton said, "my relationship with Selina is exactly the same as if Annette were here with me."

"I accept that, having met Selina," Lord Howdrith said. "But I have a feeling, if you will not think it impertinent of me to say so, that your position, Tiverton, is somewhat precarious. I should like to offer Selina my protection."

For the moment there was absolute silence and then Quintus Tiverton said:

"The only protection for Selina that I would accept would be that of a wedding-ring."

It was Lord Howdrith's turn to stiffen and after a moment he said:

"Do you really expect to find her a husband moving in the particular circles in which we have met?"

"Selina is a lady, as you must see for yourself," Quintus Tiverton replied. "Her parents, who are dead, were eminently respectable."

"Nevertheless, on your introduction, she is consorting with the *'Grandes horizontales'* of Paris."

"She will take little harm from that as long as I am looking after her," Quintus Tiverton said, and his voice was hard.

"That is, of course, a matter of conjecture," Lord Howdrith replied. "I would be very generous to Selina. I am even prepared to settle some money on her."

Quintus Tiverton rose to his feet.

"There is nothing more to discuss," he said sharply. "I am determined to find Selina a husband, although ultimately of course the choice rests with her. But I can assure you on her behalf that she would not contemplate for one moment any other relationship."

He paused to add:

"The reason she is with me at the moment is that she was frightened by a French swine who offered her the same proposition as yours."

Lord Howdrith also rose to his feet, but he made no motions to leave. Instead he walked across the small Salon and back again before he said:

"I am a very rich man, Tiverton, and I am convinced that I can give Selina far more security and far more comfort than you are able to do."

"And when you are tired of her, what then?" Quintus Tiverton enquired.

"She will be financially independent. But I do not contemplate becoming tired of anything so beautiful for many, many years."

"Selina is not the stuff that *cocottes* are made of," Quintus Tiverton said. "She has led a very sheltered life, she knows nothing of the world. Her youth and innocence may seem very attractive to you at the moment, but when they are gone . . ."

"I have told you, I will see that she is provided with money, a house of her own in London, and certainly a carriage and horses."

Quintus Tiverton laughed and it was not a pretty sound.

"Exactly what you would offer any pretty little Opera singer or *demi-mondaine* who took your fancy," he sneered. "Good God, man, we are talking about Selina! Have you looked at her?"

"I admit she is the most beautiful creature I have ever seen," Lord Howdrith answered, "but I am not yet prepared to marry anyone. I enjoy my freedom."

"Then we have nothing more to say to each other," Quintus Tiverton said. "Good-night, Howdrith. I shall advise Selina not to accept your invitation to take her driving tomorrow afternoon. She has had many other invitations and some of them should be definitely more to her advantage."

"You mean there is someone else?" Lord Howdrith asked.

"The answer to that question must be very obvious," Quintus Tiverton replied. "May I remind you once again, we are talking about Selina."

He paused to add contemptuously:

"If you will look in the Hall as you go out, you will see the enormous number of cards which have been left here this afternoon, and I imagine there are quite a number more at the Stephanie because not everyone knows we have moved."

Quintus Tiverton opened the door as he spoke but Lord Howdrith did not pass through it.

"Try to be reasonable about this, Tiverton," he said. "I should like to speak to Selina herself."

"There is nothing for you to say to her," Quintus Tiverton replied, "and I will not have you upsetting her. But I can tell you one thing: she would have been extremely shocked, if not disgusted, if she had happened to overhear the conversation we have just had about her."

He drew in his breath before he said in a voice that was like a whip-lash:

"Selina is not a piece of merchandise to be sold over the counter, or a horse to be bought by the highest bidder. Good-night, Howdrith, and do not trouble to come here again."

As he spoke Quintus Tiverton crossed the small Hall and pulled open the front door.

Lord Howdrith's carriage was waiting outside and a footman sprang from the box.

There was nothing His Lordship could do but walk down the steps and into his carriage, and he had no sooner entered it than Quintus Tiverton shut the front door, not even waiting to see him drive away.

He stood for a moment in the Hall, and then as he reached up to lower the gas-lights Selina appeared at the top of the stairs.

"I heard His Lordship go," she said. "What did he want?"

Quintus Tiverton looked up at her.

She was wearing a very simple white cotton wrapper that she herself had made.

Without the expensive elegance of her evening-gown and with her fair hair streaming over her shoulders she looked very young and inexpressibly lovely.

He did not answer her and after a moment Selina came down the stairs.

"What did he want?" she asked again.

Without looking at her Quintus Tiverton walked from the Hall and into the Salon to start extinguishing the lights there.

"It was nothing of importance," he said. "Go to bed, Selina."

She stood, hesitating, watching him as he moved about the room. Then she said in a low voice:

"He wanted to speak to ... you about ... me, did he not?"

"Why should you think that?" Quintus Tiverton questioned.

"It was something he said today which surprised me," Selina said. "He was very different from what he was last night."

"What did he say to you?" Quintus Tiverton asked.

She thought that there was an angry note in his voice and she looked up at him appealingly as she answered:

"It was not exactly what he said, it was just an impression I had. He does not want to marry me, does he?"

"No, he does not want that," Quintus Tiverton replied.

Selina looked at him. Then after a moment in a very low voice she asked:

"Did he suggest anything else?"

"I refuse to discuss it," Quintus Tiverton said abruptly. "Howdrith is of no importance in your life. Forget about him. There are plenty of other men who will pay court to you; who will be only too ready to dance with you; to offer you their hospitality; but the matter of finding you a husband is not as urgent as it was."

"Oh, I am glad . . . so very . . . very glad!" Selina said. "And if we are not extravagant I am sure that the money will last for a very long time."

"No money lasts for long," Quintus Tiverton said, "but at least we have a small amount to fall back on, and I shall not feel every time I put a sovereign on the table that it means we may have to go without luncheon or dinner."

"Could we not just . . . enjoy ourselves for a few days without your having to . . . gamble?" Selina asked hesitatingly.

"I wish the answer could be yes," Quintus Tiverton replied, "but unfortunately it is the only way I know of making money, and, let me say again, what I have won tonight will not last forever."

He saw the expression on Selina's face and then looked away from her to continue:

"Soon the Season here will be over. Everyone will be returning to Paris."

"Must we . . . must we go to . . . Paris?" Selina asked.

He knew that she was thinking of the Marquis and he replied:

"There are other cities but not such attractive ones."

"Why cannot we go to England?" Selina asked.

There was a silence and then Quintus Tiverton said:

"Because it is impossible for me to return home and I suppose I ought to tell you why."

"There is no reason why you should, if you do not wish to," Selina said quickly.

"Then let us leave things as they are," he answered. "Confessions are always unpleasant and in most cases boring. Instead let me ask you to trust me to do what is best for both of us."

"You know I trust you," Selina said, "and I have no wish to pry into your private life. You know that I am just . . . happy to be with . . . you."

There was a little catch in her voice as she spoke and now Quintus Tiverton looked at her—at her small, heart-shaped face raised to his, at her blue eyes troubled and worried, at her fair hair shining in the light of the one gas-globe he had not extinguished.

In her heel-less slippers she seemed small and somehow insubstantial, a part of a dream, and there was something spiritual and ethereal about her beauty which Quintus Tiverton could never remember having found in any other woman.

"I do not wish to be a nuisance to you," Selina said, and her lips seemed to tremble a little as she spoke. "You have been so kind, so unbelievably . . . wonderful to me. I want only what you want . . . whatever it might be."

"What I want and what I have to do are very different things," Quintus Tiverton said.

"Why?" Selina enquired.

"Because I have to think about you," he answered, "because your whole life, your whole future, depends on what happens now. I could never forgive myself if you were hurt or unhappy."

"I am happy . . . so very . . . very happy, so long as I can be with . . . you," she answered.

She spoke with an intensity which made her instinctively put out her hands towards him. They were close to each other and she had the feeling that if she could touch him he might put his arms round her again and hold her close.

She wanted to be close to him; she wanted it with every nerve in her body. There was an inexpressible longing within her which seemed to push her towards him.

And then abruptly he said in a voice that was unnaturally loud and almost rough:

"Will you go to bed, Selina! It is too late for you to be down here being a nuisance when you should be asleep. You have to look beautiful tomorrow, or have you forgotten why we are in Baden-Baden?"

If he had slapped her in the face his words and the way he spoke them could not have been more of a shock.

Her hands dropped to her sides, and as she felt the tears well into her eyes she turned and ran away from him.

She crossed the Hall to climb the stairs slowly, and only as she reached the top step did she hear him running up after her to catch up with her as she reached the landing.

"Forgive me, forgive me, Selina," he said. "I should not have spoken to you like that, but sometimes you try me too hard."

She turned her head towards him but she could not see him for the tears that were misting her eyes.

"I am grateful," he said abjectly, "overwhelmingly grateful for what you have done tonight. Tomorrow we will talk about ourselves, but not now, not here. Not when you look like that."

There was a fierce note overlying his words which she did not understand. Then suddenly he walked across the landing, opened the door to his bed-room, passed through it, and slammed it behind him.

She stood staring after him in bewilderment.

What had she said? What had she done? Why was he so upset?

She could not understand why, when they had been so happy before Lord Howdrith had arrived, everything had suddenly gone wrong.

She went into her own room and sat down on the bed.

"I love him!" she told herself in a whisper. "If I have to . . . marry someone else . . ."

At the thought of what lay ahead of her the tears ran down her cheeks. Then she reminded herself that Quintus Tiverton had not yet found a husband for her and until he did they could be together.

It was inexpressible happiness to think of him, even though the future was dark and frightening. It was also a reprieve to know that the unknown husband had not yet appeared, and that he was not Lord Howdrith.

With commendable self-control Selina did not cry herself to sleep, but she woke several times in the night as if to make quite sure that she was still in the Villa and that Quintus Tiverton was not far away from her.

She kept telling herself that she must savour and enjoy every moment that they were together.

She had the feeling that it would be these memories which would sustain and comfort her all her life and that here, in this small Villa, lay the greatest happiness she would ever know.

Yet because youth is naturally optimistic she ran downstairs to help Jim prepare Quintus Tiverton's breakfast, feeling irrepressibly gay.

It was a new day, they had money, and she was quite certain that she would be able to spend some time at any rate with Quintus Tiverton.

Selina had cooked a very elaborate breakfast by the time Quintus Tiverton came downstairs.

Jim, by some magic of his own, had already bought crisp, fresh bread, croissants, and a comb of the Black Forest honey.

There was creamy golden butter, coffee that smelt delicious, and dishes of fish, eggs, and kidneys; the latter, Jim informed Selina, being one of his Master's favourite dishes.

Looking immaculate and, in Selina's estimation, very handsome, Quintus Tiverton entered the Breakfast-Room with a smile on his lips.

"I had a feeling you were cooking for me," he said. "Not only could I smell delicious aromas floating up the stairs, but I could also hear you laughing. Meals that are prepared with laughter are, I confidently believe, always the best!"

"Jim was telling me of some of your adventures in the past," Selina said.

"I will wring his neck if he is indiscreet," Quintus Tiverton replied, but he was, Selina thought with gladness, in an exceedingly good humour.

While they were having breakfast there was a rat-tat at the door and they could hear Jim moving things about in the Hall. After some minutes he came into the Dining-Room to say:

"There's enough flowers, Sir, conveyed here from the Stephanie to set up shop, a basket from another gentleman, and a whole pile of notes! If I'm not mistaken, you won't be takin' any meals 'ere today."

He put a number of envelopes down in front of Quintus Tiverton as he spoke.

Because she was curious Selina rose from the table to look into the Hall. Jim had spoken the truth when he'd said there were enough flowers to stock a shop.

Never had she seen anything so magnificent! The huge baskets decorated with satin bows and the bouquets which were piled on tables and chairs seemed almost overpowering.

"Who could have sent me all these?" Selina enquired wonderingly.

She picked up the cards which were attached to the floral offerings as she spoke and carried them back into the Dining-Room.

"Who are your admirers?" Quintus asked.

He was slitting open the envelope he held in his hand with a pointed letter-opener which Jim had brought from the Salon.

"I have never heard of most of the people," Selina said, "but I suppose I must have been introduced to them the night before last. Oh, here is one from Lord Howdrith!"

Quintus Tiverton did not reply and after a moment she said:

"Do I write and thank him for it? It would surely be rude not to do so."

"There is no hurry," Quintus Tiverton said briefly. "Let us wait and see."

"Wait for what?" Selina asked.

"For his next move," he replied enigmatically.

He looked down at the notes which lay open on the table in front of him.

"You have certainly caused a sensation in Baden-Baden," he said. "As Jim says, there will be no necessity for us to spend money on food."

"But I like cooking for you," Selina protested, "so, please, do not accept every invitation."

"You should not be waiting on me," Quintus Tiverton said. "You should be doing nothing more exhausting than extending your hand to be kissed or listening to fulsome compliments from some lovelorn swain."

Selina laughed.

"And very nonsensical and untrue most of them are! Fortunately I do not believe any of them, and so I promise you I will not get a swollen head."

"There is every justification for you to have one," he said quietly.

Sitting at the end of the table in the morning sunshine she was, he thought, even lovelier than she had been last night.

Her dress was quite simple, but the colour became her. He had the feeling that anything Selina put on, however simple, would be transformed by some magic of her beauty into what appeared a sumptuous creation.

The expression on her face was very happy and very excited and he knew with a sudden sense of power that he could dim the radiance of her eyes with one harsh word, or wipe away her happiness by revealing a note of irritation in his voice.

'She is vulnerable,' he thought to himself, 'and far too sensitive for this type of life. And yet there is no alternative—or is there?'

"Selina," he asked, "what do you feel about Lord Howdrith?"

"Why do you ask that?" she enquired. "I thought we were not going to see him again."

"It is possible for you to do so, should you wish it," Quintus Tiverton answered.

"He is quite pleasant," she said, "but I do not wish to go with him if I can be with you."

Quintus Tiverton did not answer and she said:

"I thought from what you said last night that he was unlikely to ask me again."

Quintus Tiverton again made no reply. He had reached almost to the bottom of the pile of letters which Jim had put in front of him, and now he stared down at one with a strange look on his face before he said:

"Here is a letter for you, and if I am not mistaken it is from Howdrith."

He held it out to her and for a moment Selina was reluctant to take it.

"How do you know it is from him?" she enquired.

"It must have come with the flowers," he said, "and it is from the Stephanie. I think Lord Howdrith is the only person we know who is staying there at the moment."

Almost reluctantly Selina took the letter from his hands. She had the feeling that it contained something she did not want to hear. She did not know why, but she had an impulse to tear up the letter or refuse to open it.

But because Quintus Tiverton was obviously waiting and because really there was nothing else she could do, she opened the flap slowly and pulled out the sheet of writing-paper that was inside the envelope.

"What does he say?" Quintus Tiverton asked.

There was a note of impatience in his voice as Selina looked down at the note she held in her hand. Then she read aloud:

"My dear Selina,

"I am very anxious to talk with you and would be glad if I might call on you about noon and see you alone.

"Please do not refuse this request as it is of the utmost importance to me and, I hope, to you.

"I remain,
Yours admiringly,
Howdrith."

Selina's voice died away and then she raised her eyes to look at Quintus Tiverton on the other side of the table.

"What does this . . . mean?" she asked. "What does Lord Howdrith . . . wish to . . . say to me?"

There was a pause and then Quintus Tiverton replied dryly:

"I have a suspicion that our gamble has come off."

"What do you . . . mean by . . . that?" Selina asked.

"I will be truthful with you," Quintus replied. "Last

night Lord Howdrith suggested to me that he should become your protector."

He saw Selina go very pale and he said:

"It was not quite so insulting a suggestion as it might seem. You see, he happened to have met my real sister in England."

"Oh!" Selina ejaculated, "so he thought . . ."

"I think he assumed at first that we meant something very intimate to each other," Quintus Tiverton said, "but I put him right on that score and told him that I was in fact only your guardian."

"He . . . believed you?"

"I think he did, not because I was telling the truth but because he had seen you."

Selina looked puzzled.

"You look far too innocent and too pure to be anything but what you appear to be," Quintus Tiverton said.

"But you told him . . . you told him . . . that I could . . . not do as he . . . suggests?"

"I made it absolutely clear."

"Then why has he written to me?" Selina asked in a frightened voice. "Do you imagine that he intends to try to . . . persuade me?"

"I am quite certain that he intends to offer you marriage," Quintus Tiverton replied.

"Marriage?" Selina exclaimed. "But he . . . cannot be in love with me! He has only met me three times, and one could hardly count last night."

"You are very beautiful, Selina! Unless I am mistaken, Howdrith would not wish to lose you to anyone else."

"There is . . . no-one else," Selina said.

"There are a great many probabilities, judging by the flowers outside and the invitations we have received," Quintus Tiverton said. "I also made Howdrith believe that he is not the only horse in the race."

Selina was quiet and then she said:

"I have the feeling that you . . . pushed him into thinking that he must . . . marry me. If that is the truth . . . I would not wish to . . . accept any man in such . . . circumstances."

Quintus Tiverton pushed back his chair.

"My dear Selina, you must realise that a man like Howdrith is a matrimonial catch. There is not a match-making mother in the whole of England who would not welcome him as a son-in-law. That he has evaded their wiles and the traps they have set for him is due, I am quite convinced, to the fact that up to now his heart has never been involved."

"Are you ... saying that he might be ... falling in love with ... me?" Selina asked incredulously.

"I am almost certain that that is exactly what has happened," Quintus Tiverton said, "and the fact that he could not get you on his own terms has made it imperative for him to accept mine."

"I do not ... want him like that," Selina said. "I do not want to marry anyone who is forced into asking me to be his wife, who would rather ... if he had the choice ... have me as his ... mistress."

She blushed and the colour rose in her cheeks, making her look even lovelier than she had been before, although the blue of her eyes was like a stormy sea.

"Beggars cannot be choosers," Quintus Tiverton said dryly. "You need a husband, and let me make this quite clear, Selina, I would never have aspired on your behalf so high as Howdrith. He has always been very conscious of his own importance. He was insufferably conceited when we were at school together, and no amount of ragging or bullying could change his high opinion of himself."

His lips tightened before he continued:

"If His Lordship does condescend to offer you marriage, then all I can say is that we will have brought off a coup which far exceeds our success of last night."

Selina rose from the table and walked to the window. She stood with unseeing eyes looking out at the cyprus trees, the water of the fountain leaping iridescent into the blue sky, the flowers that made brilliant patches of colour against the dark green of the yew-hedges.

"I—I do not ... want to ... marry him," she said in a small, breathless little voice.

"He has not yet asked you," Quintus Tiverton replied.

"But he ... might do so," she answered, "and if he does ... what am I to say?"

"You will say yes," Quintus Tiverton said sharply, "and you will go down on your knees and thank God for such an amazing piece of good fortune!"

Selina did not speak and he went on:

"Think of the alternative. Remember what you had planned for yourself: to be employed as a companion or a Governess in some genteel household where you would have met no eligible men, and the only excitement you were likely to encounter was the lecherous advances of either the master of the house or perhaps his son."

Selina did not turn from the window and he continued:

"Can you imagine being at the beck and call of a querulous old woman or some tiresome, spoilt child; existing in a kind of no-man's land between the Drawing-Room and the servant's-hall; depending always on the whims and fancies of your employer, with nothing to look forward to except a lonely old age, penniless and without even the compensation of your beauty, once it faded."

His voice was harsh and now Selina turned and looked at him to say:

"I want ... to stay ... with you, you know that is what ... I want. I do not ... mind if we are ... poor, or even if we are ... hungry. I ... just want to be ... with you."

"It is impossible!"

"But why? Why?" Selina asked. "You were happy when you came down to breakfast and saw the dishes I had cooked for you. We were happy yesterday at luncheon-time and again at dinner."

Her eyes were pleading as she went on:

"I would not ... interfere with your gambling, and I will be very ... economical; I would save you money. You ... need not even take me to ... meet your friends if you do not ... wish to do so. I will stay in the house with Jim and look after you."

Her voice was very soft and beseeching, and although she spoke in a very low tone it seemed as if Quintus Tiverton listened intently to every word she said.

Rising from the table and picking up the opened letters which lay in front of him, he said crossly:

"There is no point in such arguments, Selina. You know as well as I do that you cannot stay with me indefinitely. Already our subterfuge has been discovered by Lord Howdrith, and if it is not Howdrith who is offering for you, do not suppose there will not be dozens of men, some proposing one thing, some another. But I do doubt if, as far as marriage is concerned, you will get a better offer."

"Are you telling me," Selina asked, "that if he does . . . offer for me . . . I have to . . . accept him?"

"You gave me your word of honour to obey me," Quintus Tiverton answered, "and I shall hold you to it. It is best for you, Selina. Get that firmly into your head and, as I have said, if Howdrith does come up to scratch, you will be an extremely lucky young woman."

As he finished speaking, Quintus Tiverton walked from the Dining-Room.

Selina watched him cross the Hall and go into the Salon, and she knew that he was going to collect the money he had won the night before.

She felt as if he had gone away from her, leaving her empty and drained of everything except for an indescribable pain which tortured her heart.

"I love him!" she told herself in sudden agony. "I love . . . him! Oh, God . . . what am I . . . to do?"

Chapter Seven

After a few moments Selina crossed the Hall and followed Quintus Tiverton into the Salon.

As she had expected, he was standing at the *secretaire*, with the drawer open, taking out some of the gold coins from where he had put them the night before.

As she came through the door he said over his shoulder:

"Call Jim, will you?"

There was no need for Selina to do so because Jim had heard his Master and came hurrying into the Salon.

"Did you want me, Sir?" he asked.

"Yes," Quintus Tiverton replied, "I want you to pay what we owe for the Villa, the dress-maker, and the tailor."

"And please give him some extra money for food," Selina interposed. "I am hoping that perhaps you will allow me to cook luncheon and also dinner for you to-day."

Quintus Tiverton did not answer but he added some further coins to the pile he had set aside for Jim, and Selina could not help realising that whether they dined at the Villa or went out depended entirely on what Lord Howdrith said when he called on her at noon.

Jim pocketed the coins and Quintus Tiverton then filled his pockets.

"I must change some of these into notes," he said. "I had best go to the Casino. It is nearer than the Bank."

"Will you be long?" Selina asked nervously.

She was nervous of being alone when Lord Howdrith called, and yet she knew that to say so would annoy Quintus Tiverton and she did not dare to put her feelings into words.

"Not very long," he replied after a moment, "but I intend to ride for a short while. I must have exercise."

Selina longed to ask if she could accompany him, but she knew that he would refuse.

She had the feeling that he wished to be alone or at any rate not to be with her, and she thought almost despairingly that he would expect her to spend the time making herself attractive for the arrival of Lord Howdrith.

Jim had brought his horse to the front door. Walking from the Salon, Quintus Tiverton picked up his hat from the hall table and said without looking at her:

"Good-bye, Selina. You had better move some of these flowers. As they are, it is almost impossible to get into the house."

"Yes, of course," Selina replied humbly.

She went to the door, watched him swing himself into the saddle, and wondered if it was possible that any man could look more attractive or more raffish.

There was something in the angle at which he wore his hat, the squareness of his shoulders, and the manner in which he sat his horse that made him, she thought, irresistibly dashing.

She watched him ride down the short drive and onto the road outside.

He did not look back.

She closed the door of the Villa with a pain in her heart, which she felt would be with her for the rest of her life.

Because he had asked it of her, she picked up one of the baskets of flowers and carried it into the Salon.

It was a very expensive tribute; for the flowers were orchids and the handle of the basket was decorated with two huge bows of satin ribbon, as good if not better than anything that embellished Selina's gowns.

She went back to fetch another floral offering. This one was arranged in the shape of a heart, and she wondered who had sent it and why a stranger should think it would please her.

She placed the flowers on every available table in the Salon, but still there were more in the Hall.

She looked round the room and thought what a

waste of money it had been for men who were complete strangers to send her flowers she did not want, and could not be expected to appreciate since she could not even remember the sender.

Yesterday she would have wondered desperately if there was any possible way of exchanging them for money with which to buy food.

Today things were different because she had managed to save Quintus from a further financial disaster last night, and the drawer in the *secretaire* contained enough money to last them for some time.

'Because of it,' Selina thought, a little warmth creeping into her heart, 'there is no hurry for me to marry Lord Howdrith, even if I have to do so eventually! For the moment I can stay here.'

She began to think of what excuses she would make to prevent there being any possibility of a speedy marriage.

Surely he would understand, she thought, that they must get to know each other better. Then with an agonising sense of shock she knew that marriage with Lord Howdrith meant that she might never see Quintus Tiverton again.

She would have to go away to England and leave him behind!

Even to think of it made a sudden feeling of panic seep over her so that she wanted to scream aloud that it was impossible! That she could not do it and that whatever the advantages of such a marriage, she would stay as she was!

Then like an icy hand squeezing her heart, she knew that Quintus Tiverton no longer wanted her.

He had brought her away from the Inn only because she had been so insistent, and he had saved her only on the condition that she would obey him.

He had said that he was thinking now of what was best for her. Was it not also best for him? He would be free again, unencumbered, and, as he had said before, with only himself to worry about.

Selina put her hands up to her eyes in a gesture of despair and as she did so she heard a sound in the Hall.

She thought it must be Jim returning.

'Perhaps he has forgotten something,' she thought.

With an effort she took her hands from her face and tried to compose her expression so that he would not notice that anything was wrong.

Then, as she turned round, she stood transfixed.

Three men were entering the room and each of them had a handkerchief pulled high over his face so that only his eyes were showing.

They advanced towards her almost silently and even as she took a step backwards and a scream rose to her lips, the man in the centre, with incredible swiftness, put a handkerchief over her mouth while the other two men gripped her by the arms.

They pulled her backwards even as she struggled ineffectually against them and sat her down on a hard upright chair.

Almost before she could realise what was happening she was gagged with a handkerchief which was tied in a knot at the back of her head; her wrists were tied behind her back, and a rope encircled her waist and her knees, making her completely captive to the chair.

With terrified eyes Selina watched the men move away from her side and begin to search the room.

One man pulled open the doors of a French chest which stood between the windows, another went to the *secretaire*.

He pulled out the small drawers that stood above the flap and threw them on the floor. Then he began to open the drawers beneath! The second one was locked.

The third man had turned to go upstairs, but the man at the *secretaire* called out, "Carl!" and he came back into the Salon.

A long, thin weapon was produced from the third man's pocket. He inserted it above the lock in the *secretaire* and there was the sound of wood splintering as the drawer was forced open.

Although the men did not speak there was a low guttural sound of satisfaction as they saw what was in the drawer.

In a few seconds, it seemed to Selina, they had filled

their pockets with the gold and, without even glancing in her direction, left the Salon.

She heard the kitchen door close and realised that that was the way they had entered the Villa.

Then there was only silence.

It had all happened so quickly that she could hardly believe it had really occurred and had not been an illusion.

Only the open drawer with its broken lock and the smaller drawers from the *secretaire* scattered on the floor told her that she had not been dreaming.

It had actually happened and now once again Quintus Tiverton was without money, except for what he had taken with him to change into notes at the Casino.

Selina struggled to free herself from her bonds but found it impossible.

She had been tied up very effectively and to struggle only made it hard to breathe through the handkerchief that was pulled very tightly over her nose and mouth.

She tried to calculate how long it would be before Quintus Tiverton or Jim returned to release her. But the fact that she was a prisoner was unimportant beside the knowledge that they had not been so clever after all.

The Baron had won!

It was quite obvious that it was the Baron who had sent his servants or had hired thieves to get back the money Selina and Quintus Tiverton had prevented him, last night, from winning by cheating.

Too late, Selina thought how foolish they had been to think that the Baron would not try to take his revenge in one way or another.

He was not the type of man, she thought, to be outwitted. When he'd found that a pair of his spectacles were missing he would have remembered that she had given Quintus Tiverton a pair to wear just before he began to deal the last three hands.

Three hands which Quintus had won simply because, like his host, he knew from the marked cards what his opponent's hand contained!

Wildly Selina wondered if it would be possible to

turn the tables on the Baron once again. Then she was sure that it was hopeless.

There was no proof that he was in any way connected with the theft of the gold. It would even be difficult to prove that he had cheated the night before, because she was certain that he would be astute enough to destroy the marked cards and the luminous paint just in case Quintus should talk of what had occurred.

'He is cleverer than we are,' Selina thought despairingly, and realised how uncomfortable she was and how the rope was chafing her imprisoned wrists.

Time went by very slowly, and all the while she was thinking of Quintus and what a blow this would be to him.

It had been such a relief to know that for a little while at least they need not be afraid. There was only one blessing and that was that Jim had paid their debts.

Every minute seemed an hour. There was only the tick of a gold clock on the mantelpiece until suddenly there was the sound of a carriage drawing up to the door.

'Lord Howdrith!' Selina thought as she heard the horses come to a stand-still.

The bell clanged in the kitchen.

There was no answer because Jim had not yet returned, and after a short while the footman rang again.

'Perhaps, as there is no reply, His Lordship will go away,' Selina thought optimistically, hoping that Jim would not return in time to open the door to him.

Then she heard a voice she recognised and knew that Quintus had returned and that he was speaking to Lord Howdrith.

She could hear their voices talking together and then there was silence and she guessed that Quintus had gone round to the back of the Villa to enter by the kitchen door.

The thieves had shut her into the Salon when they left and now she could not see Quintus cross the Hall to open the front door, but she heard him.

"Come in!" he said. "My servant must be out shopping, and I cannot think where Selina is. But if you will wait in the Salon I will see if I can find her."

A second later he opened the door.

Selina saw the astonishment on both men's faces as they hurried across the room to release her.

It was Quintus who unknotted the handkerchief at the back of her head and she drew in a deep breath of air before she could speak.

"What has happened? Who has done this to you?" he asked in an angry voice.

"There were ... three men," Selina answered, and her voice was barely above a whisper. "They wore handkerchiefs over their faces. They took ... everything that was in the ... drawer of the *secretaire*."

As she was speaking Lord Howdrith undid the cord that held her wrists and unwound it from her body.

She tried to stand up and realised as she did so how weak she felt. She almost fell and Quintus Tiverton's arms went round her.

"You are faint. I will get you some brandy."

"I will get it," Lord Howdrith said.

"You will find it in the Dining-Room," Quintus Tiverton told him.

As Lord Howdrith went from the room he helped Selina to the sofa, laying her head back against the satin cushions.

"They have ... taken the money ... all of it!" Selina faltered.

"I can see that," he said grimly. "They did not hurt you?"

"No ... they only tied me up ... but it was very ... frightening."

"I am sure it was."

Lord Howdrith came hurrying back into the Salon with a glass of brandy in his hand.

Quintus Tiverton took it from him and held it to Selina's lips.

"Sip it slowly!" he commanded.

She did as she was told and felt the fiery liquid sear its way down her throat.

"No ... more," she begged.

"One more sip," Quintus Tiverton insisted. "You look very pale. I think you should go and lie down."

Selina sipped the brandy as he had told her, and then as the feeling of faintness vanished she said:

"I think I will do as you suggest. It has been rather an . . . ordeal."

"Of course it has," Lord Howdrith said. "I think you are very brave."

Selina rose a little unsteadily to her feet.

"You are quite sure you are all right?" Quintus Tiverton asked. "I will carry you upstairs if you like."

"No, I can manage," Selina replied.

He helped her to the door, and then as she smiled at him weakly he watched her until she had her hand on the banister.

"Go and rest, Selina," he said, "and try not to worry. It is all over now."

She did not answer and Quintus Tiverton went back into the Salon and shut the door.

As soon as he had done so, Selina crossed the Hall on tip-toe and went into the kitchen.

'It will soon be luncheon-time,' she thought. 'I must begin to prepare something for us to eat.'

She had not been in the kitchen for more than a few minutes when the back door was pushed open and Jim came in, carrying a large number of packages.

"Someone's broken the lock, Miss Selina!" he exclaimed.

"Yes, I know," Selina answered. "We have been robbed, Jim, robbed of every penny that the Master had left in the drawer!"

Jim stared at her for a moment with an almost ludicrous expression of dismay on his face, and then putting the packages down on the table he said:

"It's always the same—easy come, easy go! It's a good thing the Master had some of the money with him."

"And that you have paid the bills," Selina said.

"Yes, that's true, Miss," Jim agreed. "But we're back again where we were before."

"That is just what I was thinking," Selina said despairingly.

It was a little while later that she heard Quintus Tiverton seeing Lord Howdrith out.

The carriage drove away, and then as Selina thought he was about to go upstairs to look for her she called out:

"I am here if you want me!"

Quintus Tiverton came into the kitchen.

"I told you to lie down."

"I am quite all right," Selina answered, "and we have to eat. Luncheon will be ready in a few moments, and I hope you are hungry."

"I ought to reply that I am too upset," Quintus Tiverton replied, "but as a matter of fact I am prepared to enjoy anything you have to offer me."

"I am glad about that," Selina smiled.

Jim waited on them while they ate and they did not discuss what had happened until he had served the coffee and left them alone.

"Now tell me exactly what happened," Quintus Tiverton said, sitting back in his chair, his eyes on Selina's face.

"It was terrifying," Selina said. "They moved so quickly, and only one man spoke, when he called to another by the name of Carl to come and open the locked drawer."

"The Baron has been clever!" Quintus Tiverton remarked.

"That is exactly what I was thinking," Selina answered, "and we were foolish to think we could defeat him. You should have taken all the money with you."

She paused and asked:

"How much did you take?"

"About a hundred pounds in our money," he replied.

Selina gave a little sigh of relief.

"That can last us for some time."

"Not in Baden-Baden," he replied, "and it is not a question of 'us,' Selina! I have arranged with Lord Howdrith that you should be married tomorrow morning."

Selina felt as if she were turned to stone, and although she wanted to cry out that it was impossible the words would not come to her lips.

"I told Howdrith exactly how I was placed," Quintus

Tiverton said in a cold, emotionless voice, "and as it happens he wishes to marry you at once and take you away from Baden-Baden."

There was a faint twist to his lips as he added:

"His Lordship does not approve of the company I keep, not where you are concerned."

"Surely he ... wants to ... stay for the ... races?" Selina faltered.

"Surprisingly, you are more important to him than his horses," Quintus Tiverton replied. "He is arranging for the marriage to take place before the Mayor at noon, and then you will leave on the train which departs early in the afternoon on the first stage of your journey to the Hague."

"You seem to have arranged everything between you," Selina said. "Have I no say in what concerns me?"

"None!" Quintus Tiverton replied. "Howdrith has made up his mind and I have no intention of trying to dissuade him."

"But I do not ... know him," Selina said. "How can I ... marry a man I ... do not know ... and who does not know ... me?"

"It is what you told me you were prepared to do," Quintus Tiverton said in a hard voice, "and you know as well as I do there is no alternative, especially at this moment."

"But you can ... win more money," Selina persisted. "You have won ... before and you will ... win again."

"There is no guarantee I shall do anything of the sort," Quintus Tiverton replied, "but in your case, you are backing a certainty. You will be Lady Howdrith, married to a very wealthy man, and your position for the rest of your life will be unassailable."

He paused to add a little more gently:

"You will be safe, Selina. That is what matters to a woman. You will be safe."

Selina's instinct was to reply that she did not want to be safe; she did not want an important position, wealth, or a husband. But she knew that not only would Quintus Tiverton over-rule anything she said, he would also despise her for trying to break her word to him.

She had given him her word of honour. She had forced him into the position of being her guardian, and as her guardian he could make any plans he thought fit with regard to her future.

Quintus Tiverton rose to his feet.

"I am going to the Casino to see if there is a chance of increasing the money I have left."

"Can I come with you?"

"Your future husband has made it quite clear he does not wish you to appear in public. He is very conscious that your reputation as his wife must be above reproach; and I am sure when he speaks to you about it he will ask you to forget the fact that you have been a guest of Madame Leblanc, or that you were introduced to Madame Letessier."

Quintus Tiverton paused to add:

"You have your packing to do, Selina, and that should keep you occupied."

"Can we . . . dine here?" Selina asked in a very small voice.

"I have persuaded Howdrith that it might be best for you not to meet each other until I take you to the Town Hall tomorrow morning."

Quintus Tiverton walked towards the door.

"I have the feeling," he said severely, "that I cannot entirely trust you to behave as gratefully as you should towards your future bridegroom."

Selina did not answer and he said:

"I will come back for dinner; but I hope our last night together, Selina, will not be spoilt by dramatics. Quite frankly, I have no stomach for them."

Quintus Tiverton walked out of the Dining-Room and a moment later she heard the front door close behind him.

Only then did Selina give a little cry of sheer misery and put her hands up to her eyes.

Dinner was not a happy meal despite the fact that Selina had done everything possible to try to make it a memorable occasion since it was the last time she would dine with Quintus Tiverton.

She had cooked all the dishes which Jim had told her were his favourites, and she had put on one of her prettiest new gowns and arranged her hair almost as skillfully as any *coiffeur* might have done.

But she could not erase the pain in her heart, and she found it almost impossible to look at Quintus Tiverton without an expression of pleading in her eyes which told him without words how much she was suffering.

While Jim was in the room they talked of ordinary things.

Quintus Tiverton had made a little money at the Casino, only a little, but, he told Selina, he had the chance of joining a private party that evening.

"It is similar to the Baron's card-games," he explained, "with the difference, I am sure, that this will be straight. The host is a man I know well, and I would no more expect him to cheat at cards than pull his horse in a race."

"I hope you win," Selina said.

But she knew as she spoke that it would make no difference where she was concerned, because, win or lose, she had to marry Lord Howdrith.

As they finished dinner Quintus Tiverton sat for a moment staring at the glass of brandy he held in his hand, and then he said:

"In two or three days' time you will be in England."

It was just a statement, as if he was following aloud his train of thought, but Selina replied:

"Shall I . . . ever see . . . you . . . again?"

"That is a question I cannot answer," he replied. "As I told you, I cannot come to England."

"Why not?" Selina enquired.

"Do you really want to know the answer to that?"

"You know I do."

"Then I will tell you the reason why I cannot return to my own country," Quintus Tiverton said, and she knew by the way he spoke that it hurt him to speak of it.

"My father was always pressed for money," he began, "and when he retired from the Army he had little more than his pension. He was the younger brother of the Earl of Arkley, but my Uncle was extremely parsimonious and, although he himself was very wealthy, he did nothing to help my father or any of his other relations."

"Sir John Wilton said the Earl of Arkley hates you," Selina said, "but I did not like to question you about it."

"He told the truth," Quintus Tiverton replied, "and the reason he hates me is that he himself is unable to produce a son. He has three daughters and since my father is dead I am now the heir-presumptive to the title."

Selina's eyes were wide with surprise but she made no comment and Quintus Tiverton went on:

"When I left Oxford my father wished me to go into his Regiment, but I knew it was something we could not really afford, and it would have meant endless sacrifices on his part."

He sighed before he continued:

"We quarrelled because he was so insistent, and I went abroad ostensibly to make my fortune."

He smiled somewhat wryly as he said:

"I failed ignominiously to do that, but I certainly enjoyed myself."

"In . . . Paris?" Selina asked.

"I went first to Paris," Quintus Tiverton said, "and the gay city and its beautiful women were a fantastic experience for any young man."

"Even though you had no money?"

"I learnt from experts how to be very proficient at cards," Quintus Tiverton replied. "It is a precarious existence, but at least if one is clever enough one exists, and that is what I did."

'He must also have made love to many beautiful women, like Caroline Letessier,' Selina thought.

As if he read her thoughts Quintus Tiverton said:

"Even the most avaricious women can be generous with their favours to a young man. People were very kind to me, Selina."

Selina drew in her breath. It hurt her to think of what kindnesses he had received and from whom.

"I made Paris my headquarters," Quintus Tiverton went on, "but I journeyed all over Europe, Egypt, and other parts of Africa. After three years I went home, only to find that the situation was just as it had been before I left: my Uncle overbearing, my father having to toady to him for every penny."

His lips tightened before he continued:

"I disliked the situation so much that I left again and went to India. It was while I was there that I heard my father had died. I was engaged in some rather difficult business deals which I thought might turn out to be lucrative, and it was therefore impossible for me to return home at once."

He paused as if he was recalling to himself what had happened before he said:

"I did however write to my Uncle. I told him the position I was in, and asked him to find an Agent to run my father's Estate for me until I could return. I promised to send him some money besides giving him Power of Attorney while I was still abroad."

"What happened?" Selina asked.

"My business transactions turned out well," Quintus Tiverton replied. "I despatched to my Uncle nearly all the money I had made and came home as soon as I was able to do so."

He paused to look at Selina's alert little face as she listened to all he had to say.

"I found," he said slowly, "that my Uncle had, I think deliberately, employed a man as Agent for my father's Estate who was both untrustworthy and a bully."

"Oh, no!" Selina exclaimed.

"He had created absolute havoc in what had been my home," Quintus Tiverton said. "He had also spent, with my Uncle's acquiescence, I am convinced, every penny I had sent back from India."

Quintus Tiverton's voice was raw as he went on:

"I went to my Uncle and told him what I thought of him. I also said in the heat of the moment: 'I will kill this swine for the way he has treated the pensioners and those who have served my family well for years. I will kill him, and his death will be at your door!' "

Selina clasped her hands together as she drew in her breath.

"What happened?"

"The Agent, Lew Harrow, was found dead the following day!" Quintus Tiverton replied. "I had not murdered him, but my Uncle believed I had done so."

"How could he think that?" Selina asked.

"I had no convincing alibi, and I could only give my Uncle my word that while I had spoken wildly against the man who had robbed me, I would not have taken his life."

"But your Uncle did not believe you?"

"He did not wish to believe me, and he told me that if I did not leave England and stay out of the country I would be brought to trial and he would give evidence against me!"

"How could he do such a thing?" Selina cried.

"He hates me!" Quintus Tiverton replied.

"So you left England?"

"I collected what money I could, and because I knew that my Uncle was quite prepared to put his threats into action, Jim and I crossed the Channel. We decided to make our way leisurely towards Baden-Baden, where there was a chance of exploiting the only talent I have, that of being a proficient gambler."

He paused, his eyes on Selina's face.

"You know what happened! I found myself encumbered with someone who appeared to be in an even worse predicament than I was myself."

"You ... saved me," Selina said, "when you ... could not ... afford to ... do so."

"I certainly could not afford it," Quintus Tiverton agreed. "But all's well that ends well, at least where you are concerned.

"Do you really ... believe that?" Selina asked.

"I believe it!"

Quintus Tiverton rose to his feet as he spoke and added:

"Now you know my story: why I am a wanderer

over the world, unable to live in the one place I love,
the one place to which I belong."

"England!" Selina said softly.

"Yes, England!" he answered, and she heard the
pain in his voice.

Then he squared his shoulders and threw back his
head as he finished his brandy.

"What is the point of being gloomy?" he asked.
"There is still a great deal of amusement to be enjoyed,
especially where there are women. Smile, Selina, things
turn out for the best one way or another, and you at
least have everything to look forward to."

Selina did not answer. Then as Quintus Tiverton
rose to his feet she rose too.

"I have . . . something to . . . ask you," she said in a
low voice.

"What is it?" he enquired.

She did not reply and then after a moment she said,
hardly above a whisper:

"Would you . . . just for . . . t-tonight, make me . . .
your mistress . . . so that I shall . . . have something to
. . . remember?"

There was a silence and it seemed as if Quintus
Tiverton was turned to stone. Then loudly, in a voice
so harsh that it made Selina start, he replied:

"How dare you ask me such a thing! Do you think
that I want you like that? I have left you pure and innocent, and that is how you will be married
tomorrow!"

It seemed to Selina that the expression on his face
was as angry as the sound of his voice.

Then he pulled open the door, walked across the
Hall, and a moment later she heard the front door slam
behind him.

The sound seemed to echo and reecho through the
Villa until there was only silence and her own feeling
of despair.

A long time later Selina walked up the stairs, moving
like an old woman and holding on to the banister to assist her lagging footsteps.

In her bed-room were the trunks she had been packing during the afternoon.

They contained the beautiful new dresses that Quintus Tiverton had bought her in Baden-Baden, and she had thought that he would admire her in those she had not yet worn.

She had been woman enough to know that there had been a glint of admiration in his eyes when he had looked at her in every new gown she put on.

Tonight when she had come from the kitchen having prepared his meal and had taken off the apron in which she cooked, he said:

"You look as if you have stepped out of a fairy-tale, but then there is always something about you which seems unreal."

He had seen the gladness in her face at his remark and turned away quickly, as if he felt he had said too much, to take a bottle of wine from the silver cooler.

"He does admire me . . . he does!" Selina told herself. "But he will never love me . . . not as I love him."

She knew now how foolish she had been to suggest that he should make love to her just for one night before her marriage, but she longed as she had never longed for anything in her whole life to feel his lips on hers and to know that she was close to him.

She had only a vague idea of what being a mistress involved, but she was sure that if she could be to Quintus what Caroline Letessier had been, it would be a wonder and a joy beyond expression.

"I might have guessed," she told herself miserably, "that it would be against his code of honour."

She knew without being told, although she had little experience with men, that Quintus Tiverton might be a gambler and an adventurer but he would never do anything that was underhanded or dishonourable.

And she was quite sure now that he would never have cheated Lord Howdrith by taking him a bride who was not pure and innocent as he had professed her to be. It would not be the behaviour of a gentleman!

"I love him!" Selina told herself desperately. "I love everything about him: his kindness, his understanding, the way he can be both masterful and at the same time very gentle."

Vaguely she realised that if she had entrusted herself to any other man in similar circumstances she might have been as frightened and as horrified with him as she had been with the Marquis.

Quintus Tiverton had indeed treated her as if she were his real sister. And yet at times it seemed as if he had not been able to prevent a caressing note in his voice, just as he could not hide the glint of admiration in his eyes.

"I love him so much ... how can I be without him?" Selina asked herself.

She did not cry, she felt as if she was past tears. She was just numb to the point of misery, feeling as if her whole body had turned to ice and she would never be warm or happy again.

"Perhaps if I feel like this," she told herself, "I shall not mind Lord Howdrith touching me. I shall not even care if he kisses me."

And yet she knew that even to think of it sent a little shudder through her body—not that he was repulsive as the Marquis had been, but at the same time, she felt that even to think of him was to withdraw into herself.

It was the very opposite of what happened when she thought of Quintus Tiverton. Then she felt as if she expanded like a flower towards the sun. She wanted to throw out her arms; to open her heart; to give him not only her lips but also her very soul.

"All through my life," Selina told herself, "I shall have only this to remember. These moments when we have been together; these precious days; these hours; these minutes when I have been able to talk to him; when I could hear his voice and watch his face."

She knew then that when she left him behind tomorrow part of herself would remain with him.

It would be only an empty shell who would journey to England with Lord Howdrith; who would be called "M'Lady" by the servants; who would sit at the other end of his table and bear his children.

At the thought of it Selina gave a little cry, and then

with an almost super-human effort at self-control she forced back the tears that came to her eyes.

It was all hopeless! Utterly and completely hopeless!

There was nothing she could do to alter her life. She would just have to endure what had to be endured until she died.

Slowly, almost without thinking, she undressed.

She picked up her new gown in which Quintus had admired her and placed it on the top of her trunk.

All her night-gowns were packed except the one she would wear tonight. She put it over her head and let down her hair so that it fell in a shining cloud over her shoulders.

She turned out the gas-lights, leaving one candle alight beside her bed, then as she had done ever since she had been a child she knelt down to say her prayers.

The formal prayers she normally said seemed inappropriate tonight and so she prayed from her heart:

"Please, God . . . take care of Quintus . . . let him be happy . . . and one day let him be able to return to England. Take care of him . . . please, God . . . take care of him . . . because I love him so . . . desperately."

She prayed for a long time, saying the same words over and over again, and then when there seemed to be no more to say she felt as if even God had ceased to listen to her pleas.

She went on kneeling there, her hands outstretched over the bed; her fingers linked together; her face hidden against the blankets.

She felt as if every second that passed was taking her farther and farther away from Quintus. She felt as if tomorrow she would leave the sunshine behind and there would be only darkness.

"How can I bear it? How can I live without him?"

She said the words out loud and then suddenly she started to her feet.

It was no use! She had tried to face the future, but it was impossible! Impossible to be without him, impossible to be the wife of another man.

What did it matter what anybody thought? She was utterly unimportant, of so little consequence in the world.

She walked to the wardrobe and took down the travelling-cloak that she had left out in case she needed it for the train. It was the same one in which she had carried her few possessions from the Inn.

She clasped it over her night-gown, then almost as if she walked in a dream she moved across the room and went slowly down the stairs.

'It must be late,' she thought, 'because the lights are out in the kitchen.'

There was only one gas-globe, turned very low, left burning in the Hall.

She walked to the front door. It was unbolted for Quintus's return and he had a key with which to let himself into the house.

Most gentlemen expected their servants to wait up for them, but Quintus, as Selina knew, was always very considerate of Jim, and took the key with him.

Just for a moment she hesitated.

She knew that what she was about to do was wicked and was a sin in the eyes of the Church; but even if it meant she was condemned to Hell in the next world, she knew she could not go on living in this.

That would be a Hell beyond endurance, a Hell so agonising, so utterly terrifying, that she could not contemplate it.

With a sound that was like a little sob she put out her hands to open the door and as she did so she gave a frightened gasp.

Standing facing her with the key in his hand was Quintus Tiverton.

Chapter Eight

For a moment neither of them moved and then Quintus Tiverton asked sharply:

"Where are you going?"

It seemed as if Selina's voice had died in her throat and she could only stare at him, her eyes very wide in her pale face.

"Tell me!" he demanded. "Where were you going?"

He stepped forward as he spoke, so that instinctively she moved before him back into the house.

As if he compelled her to answer him she replied in a voice that he could hardly hear:

"T-to ... the ... river."

He was very still and his expression was incredulous as if he could not believe what he had heard. Then something seemed to snap in Selina, and as her hands went out towards him she cried incoherently:

"It is ... no use! I ... cannot ... marry him. I love ... you! Without you I do not ... want to go on ... living. Let me ... go! L-let me ... destroy myself. There is ... no other ... way!"

Her voice broke as the tears poured down her face and her words were almost unintelligible.

Then with a swift movement, as if she would pass him, Selina moved towards the still-open door.

Quintus Tiverton caught hold of her as she took the first step and slammed the door closed. Then as he held her close against him she burst into a tempest of weeping.

"I ... love ... you!" she sobbed through her tears. "I love you ... and I could not ... bear another ... man to ... touch me."

Quintus Tiverton picked her up in his arms and carried her up the stairs.

153

She was still crying frantically, frighteningly, as he laid her down on her bed, and he remembered how she had cried in the same way when he had gone to her attic-room because the sound had disturbed him.

Now it seemed as if her tears were even more agonising as she lay against the pillows, her eyes closed and the tears running from beneath her lashes down her face.

"L-let me . . . go," she whispered, "let me go!"

There was a strange expression on his face as he looked down at her. Then with something like a groan he bent forward and kissed her.

For a moment she was still with the surprise of it, until as his lips moved on hers she felt a sudden rapture!

It was a wonder such as she had never known and it seeped over her, to sweep away her tears and the awareness of anything except Quintus himself.

His mouth was at first rough, as if his self-control had broken and he was compelled, against his will, to kiss her.

Then as he felt the softness of her lips, as he felt her quiver beneath the thin lawn of her night-gown, his mouth became more possessive, more demanding, and at the same time tender.

To Selina it was as if the Heavens had suddenly opened and shone their light on her when she had been lost in the utter darkness of despair.

Her whole body came alive, and in a kiss that joined her completely and forever to Quintus Tiverton she gave him both her heart and soul.

He kissed her until she was no longer aware of where she was or that the world existed outside themselves. It was a rapture and an ecstasy beyond anything she had ever dreamt, beyond imagination.

He took his lips from her mouth to kiss her eyes and her cheeks, still wet from her tears. He kissed her forehead and then her neck, feeling the little pulse beating excitedly because she thrilled at the touch of his mouth.

Then his lips were on hers again, taking possession of her; making her completely and absolutely his captive; so that she felt as if she surrendered herself to him, body, mind, and spirit.

Finally, when time had stood still, he raised his head to say hoarsely:

"I tried to do what I thought best for you, my beautiful darling, but you tried me too hard."

"I love ... you! Oh, Quintus ... I love ... you!" she murmured.

And in the candle-light he knew that he had never seen a woman look so radiant, so utterly and ecstatically happy.

"This is madness," he said, "you know that!"

"Divine ... wonderful ... glorious madness!" she answered. "I knew it would be like Heaven for you to kiss me, but this is beyond Heaven itself!"

"Oh, my God!" he said almost beneath his breath, "I cannot let you go! I had to steel myself to lose you, Selina, but you have tempted me and now it is too late!"

"You ... love me?" she asked in a whisper.

"I have loved you, I think, since the first moment I saw you," he answered. "I never knew a woman could be so divinely beautiful and so perfect in every way."

"Do you mean that?" she asked.

He answered her with a kiss which seemed once again to take her heart from between her lips so that it was no longer hers. Then with an effort he released her and sat back.

"We have to talk, my precious," he said, "and if you will allow me, I will put on something more comfortable."

He rose to his feet but Selina's hands went out towards him.

"You will not leave me?"

"I find it impossible to do so," he answered with a twist of his lips. "Get into bed, Selina, it is difficult for me to talk sensibly when you look as you do now."

For the first time she realised that her cloak had fallen from her shoulders when he had lain her down on the bed and her night-gown was very transparent.

She blushed, and as Quintus went from the room she slipped between the sheets to lean back against the pillows, feeling that her happiness lit the room with a glory that had not been there before.

Quintus had left the door open and she could hear him moving about in his bed-room.

A few minutes later he came back into the room wearing a long silk robe, the frills of his night-shirt showing white against his brown skin. It made him, she thought, look younger, and at the same time, if possible, even more attractive.

He crossed the room and sat down on the side of the bed to look at her—her huge eyes shining as if there were a light inside her, and her lips warm from his kisses curved in a smile.

"What have you done to me?" he asked.

"Have I not made you happy?"

"I feel drunk with a happiness I did not know existed! I am telling you the truth, Selina, when I say I have never before felt like this in my whole life."

"I am glad . . . so very glad," she answered. "I have been so . . . jealous of all the beautiful women you have loved in the past. I thought that I could never attract you as they have done."

"You are the one and only woman in my life who has ever mattered to me," he answered. "But because I love you as I have never loved before, I tried to do what was right for you."

"How could you send me away . . . when I am yours?" she asked. "How can I give another man what belongs to you?"

Quintus Tiverton drew a deep breath. He took Selina's hand which lay on the sheet in his, and held it very tightly, staring at her long, thin fingers as he said:

"Have you really considered what will happen to you if you stay with me? You have the chance, Selina, of a very comfortable, secure life, with a man of considerable importance in the social world."

"Do you really think any of that matters?" Selina asked.

"Perhaps not at the moment," Quintus Tiverton said, "but can you stand years of wondering where your next meal will come from, journeying from gambling Spa to gambling Spa, moving between Mansion and attic, and having when things were really desperate to pawn everything you possess, perhaps even your wedding-ring?"

His voice was low and grave and then as he finished speaking Selina laughed.

"How foolish you are!" she said. "Do you really think that any of that matters beside the fact that we shall be together? That I can love you and look after you and that however difficult or frightening things are, we will still have each other?"

"Oh, my darling," he said, "when you talk like that I believe you. But some part of my brain stands aside from the emotions you arouse in me and tells me that I am being selfish."

"I am the one who is selfish," Selina said. "I came into your life and disrupted it. I forced myself upon you and now, though I know you would fare better without me, I cannot leave you."

"Do you think I want you to do that?" Quintus asked with a sudden depth of passion in his voice.

He looked again into her eyes and she saw the fire in his and knew that the flame flickered within her because she desired him even as he desired her.

He did not kiss her as she had expected him to do, but said in the same grave voice in which he had spoken before:

"Can I really ask you to stay with me, knowing there will be times when the anxiety and the penury in which we have to live may take their toll even on your beauty?"

His lips tightened before he said:

"Supposing then you reproach me, not in words, because I know you would never do that, but because I should see that your clothes were shabby and your hands work-worn and sore from slaving for me."

"I should still love you," Selina answered with a little catch in her breath, "and as long as you love me, everything we experience together will be a wonderful adventure."

"Oh, my precious, my precious! You make it very hard for me to do what I know is right."

"It is right for me to be with you," Selina said. "We belong to each other. Do you not believe that?"

"Of course I believe it!" he said roughly. "You were mine from the first moment I saw you and I knew without realising it you were the woman I had been seeking to find all my life."

"When were you sure of that?" Selina asked.

As if he could not help himself Quintus smiled at her.

"I think it was when I came into that attic in the morning and found you even more beautiful than I remembered."

Selina drew in her breath with happiness and he went on:

"I had been half afraid that it had been a trick of the candle-light, but in the sunshine you were as exquisite as the sun itself."

His voice deepened as he added:

"I loved you then and that love has grown until it has become an agony beyond words not to make you mine."

"And . . . now?" Selina asked almost beneath her breath.

He looked at her and saw what she asked of him.

"We will be married as soon as we reach Paris."

"P-Paris?" Salina faltered.

"We will catch the early train tomorrow morning," he answered. "I think there is an express at about seven o'clock. I will leave a letter for Howdrith—I owe him that."

"Y-you need not . . . marry me, if you do not . . . wish to," Selina whispered.

"You have already made that suggestion to me once tonight," Quintus replied. "If you make it again I shall be very angry!"

"I would not . . . wish to . . . tie you."

"I am tied," he answered. "I am tied to you, my darling, by every instinct and emotion that a man is capable of feeling. You are mine and I want you, not only as a woman but as my wife, Selina, and please, God, one day as the mother of my children."

Selina gave a little cry of sheer happiness and now as

if she could not help herself she held out her arms to him.

He rose to lie down beside her on top of the bed and pull her close against him so that her head was on his shoulder.

His lips were on her hair and then her forehead and she could feel his heart beating frantically against the softness of her breast.

"You are . . . not angry, are you?" she asked after a moment.

"Only in that you should under-rate the love I have for you," he replied. "I understood tonight, my sweet, what you meant when you asked if I would take you as my mistress, and I knew it came from the depth of your heart. But I could not despoil anything so perfect, nor would I destroy the ideals which I know you and I both hold."

"I am . . . sorry," Selina said humbly.

"I have to be strong for both of us," Quintus said, "and therefore, while I intend to lie here with you tonight, my precious, until it is time for us to rise, I shall not make you mine until you are my wife, both in the eyes of the Law and in the sight of God."

There was something so solemn in the way he spoke, and yet so moving, that Selina felt the tears come into her eyes.

"I shall . . . pray that I shall be as you . . . want me to be," she said. "You know that I am very . . . ignorant about many things, and you must be patient with me."

"You are very young," Quintus Tiverton said, "and I adore both your innocence and your ignorance. There are so many things I want to teach you, my darling one, and to do so will be an experience I have never had before."

Selina looked up at him, not understanding, and he went on:

"You know, because I have told you, that I have found amusement always with sophisticated women; those who have made Paris the gayest and most talked-about city in the world."

"That is what makes me so afraid," Selina said.

Quintus smiled.

"That is one thing you need never be. It is because you are so different! Your purity, my beloved, shines like a light in the darkness, so that I am prepared not only to love you but to worship at your feet."

Selina gave a little murmur and hid her face against him.

When he spoke to her like this, with that note in his voice she had never heard before, her happiness was almost unbearable.

Quintus put his fingers under her chin and turned her face to his.

"I love you!" he said. "Why are there no words in any language to express my true feelings? Even the expression 'love' seems inadequate at this particular moment."

He kissed her very gently. She felt now that there was a dedication in his kiss, and while a flame flickered within her so that she felt the same rapture seeping through her body there was also a certain sanctity that had not been there before.

"I am so happy!" she whispered when he released her lips. "I feel as if I could die because everything is so wonderful."

He held her tightly.

"You are going to live for me from now until eternity," he answered fiercely, "because I will never let you go."

They talked and kissed through the hours of darkness. Sometimes they dozed a little and then awoke to seek each other.

Sometimes the fire burning so fiercely in Quintus seemed to consume them both so that Selina thought he must possess her physically and make her his.

But his self-control never broke and only once he released her to lie breathing quickly, his heart almost bursting from his breast.

"Should . . . you . . . leave . . . me?" Selina questioned shyly.

"No, my sweetest," he replied. "But your beauty—

your softness—and your lips would drive any man insane!"

"I am . . . sorry!"

"I doubt it," he replied. "You wanted to enslave me
and you have succeeded. I am your captive, Selina, and
a very willing one."

Then he turned towards her and kissed her until she
could no longer breathe or think, but only feel and
feel. . . .

When the first light of dawn showed beneath the curtains Quintus said:

"Soon we must get up. I will wake Jim and tell him
to pack my things. It is fortunate that your trunks are
ready."

"We must not miss the train," Selina said with a little
quiver of fear in her voice.

She thought that she would not feel safe until they
had left Baden-Baden and Lord Howdrith far behind.

She was still afraid that Quintus might be persuaded
at the last moment that it would be best for her to return to England in a position of social importance
rather than to wander in exile with him.

'I would follow him barefoot wherever he might wish
to go,' Selina thought to herself.

Looking up at him in the dim light coming through
the windows, she knew that it would be impossible for
any other man to attract her.

Quintus was so handsome, so irresistibly masculine
and at the same time so gentle and considerate.

Just as she had thought when he had first rescued
her that he was St. George saving her from the dragon,
so he had behaved during the night with an idealism
that could have been possible only for a man of noble
character.

Innocent though she was, Selina was well aware that
to lie all night in the arms of a man and for him to
treat her not only with respect, but also as if in some
way she was sacred, was unique.

Who would believe it, she asked herself, if she told
anyone what had occurred?

In her heart she thanked God with what was a paean

of gratitude for the happiness which had saved her at the eleventh hour.

If Quintus had returned home a few minutes later, she might at this moment be lying in the river, a soaked and senseless body from which life had been extinguished.

Instead she could think only of the joy of being his wife, knowing that nothing could ever harm her again.

While she was looking up at him, thinking how attractive he was, Quintus was looking at her.

As dawn crept up the sky and the first rays of the sun touched the hills above Baden-Baden he could see the outline of Selina's heart-shaped face; her large eyes filled with love and trust; her lips awaiting his kisses.

His arm tightened round her and then he said:

"We had better be rising, my darling. There is a great deal to do. I will go and rouse Jim."

"I expect he is awake," Selina answered. "He is a very early riser."

"I will make sure," Quintus replied. "He has to take the horses to the stable, sell them, and order a carriage to convey us to the Station."

"I will cook some breakfast as soon as I am dressed."

"I am hungry," Quintus smiled, "and I expect you are too."

"I am too happy to eat," she replied.

He would have risen from the bed when her arms went round his neck to hold him.

"I love you!" she whispered. "You have not changed your mind? You still want to marry me?"

"Once we are married," he said in a deep voice, "I will tell you how much I love you. If I start to do so now we will miss the train."

Nevertheless, he did kiss her, and for a long, long moment their bodies throbbed with their need of each other. Then with an effort Quintus released himself from Selina's arms and crossed the room to pull back the curtains.

The sunlight flooded in and he stood for a moment looking at the water from the fountain glittering like a thousand diamonds as it sparkled in the clear air.

"I had expected," he said quietly, "this to be the darkest and most miserable day of my life."

"Because I was leaving you?" Selina asked.

"Because I intended to hand you over to another man knowing that you took my heart with you and I should never again be complete."

"But now . . . ?"

"I am happy and grateful beyond words."

He turned to look at her and thought that no other woman could look so beautiful and so entirely natural in the morning light. Then, as if he forced himself to do so, he went from Selina's bed-room, closing the door behind him.

She got up, bathed in cold water, and dressed herself in the attractive silk travelling-gown that she knew would have been her wedding-dress if she had married Lord Howdrith.

Already it was too hot to put on the jacket in which she would travel, but she put everything else she possessed into her trunks, leaving out only a pretty bonnet trimmed with flowers, her gloves, and a small handbag.

Jim, she knew, would come upstairs to strap down the trunks. What was important now was that Quintus should have some breakfast.

"If we have plenty to eat now," Selina told herself, "we shall not be so hungry during the train journey, and can save money."

Already she was planning to herself how economical she would be. At the same time she was determined that where Quintus was concerned he should never, if she could help it, have anything but the very best.

She ran downstairs to find no-one in the kitchen and thought that Jim must have gone with the horses as Quintus had said he should do.

The fire, however, was already alight in the range and there was plenty of food for her to choose from.

She covered her gown with a large white apron she had worn before and started methodically and neatly to heat her pans and to prepare the food on the big table which stood in the centre of the kitchen.

Whoever had built the Villa had not forgotten that a kitchen is an important room in a house and it was attractively decorated with large wooden dressers carved by the peasants who lived in the hills.

The floor was flagged, while copper pans hung on the walls, gleaming from the polishing that Jim had given them.

Selina was well ahead with preparing the breakfast when Quintus came into the room.

He was, as usual, exceedingly smart, and she thought that she had never seen him look so happy.

"I will not be long now," she said with a smile.

"There is plenty of time," he answered.

"Why do you not wait in the Dining-Room?" she suggested. "I have an egg-dish for you to start with."

"I like watching you," he answered, "and I find it difficult to look at anything else."

She blushed at the sudden note of passion in his voice.

"You are making me shy!" she protested.

"I adore you when you are shy!"

He came nearer to the table.

"Is it permitted to kiss the cook?"

"Certainly not!" she replied severely, but at the same time she lifted her lips to his.

He put his arm round her and drew her almost roughly against him.

"I love you!" he said. "It is impossible to think of anything else except that I love you."

"That is all I want to hear," she answered softly.

His lips found hers and for a moment the kitchen whirled round them. Then the door opened and almost reluctantly they drew apart.

Jim came into the kitchen.

"Good news, Sir, I got fifty pounds for the horses."

"Excellent!" Quintus Tiverton exclaimed. "That was more than I expected."

"I'll give you the money, Sir."

Putting the packet he was carrying down on the table, Jim said:

"I saw some nice fresh trout in the market, Miss Selina, and I thought they was just what the Master'd like for his breakfast.

"Oh, thank you, Jim!" Selina exclaimed, "it will not take long to fry them."

She went on stirring the eggs as Jim handed over the money to Quintus Tiverton and then opened the package he had put down on the table.

The fish were wrapped up in a page of the local newspaper, which was printed in German.

He lifted them up and then as he placed the trout into the pan that Selina held out for him he said:

"That's funny, Sir!"

"What is?" Quintus Tiverton enquired.

"There's your name written here in this newspaper, and His Lordship's!"

"Let me see!"

Quintus Tiverton picked up the page from the table. It was stained where the fish had lain in it, but the paragraph to which Jim was referring was at the top.

"What does it say?" Selina asked in a frightened voice.

Quintus did not reply for a moment, and then as if he realised that both Selina and Jim were waiting, he slowly translated aloud:

England, September 1868

MURDERER
COMMITTED TO THE ASSIZES

The murderer of the 6th Earl of Arkley was today committed by the Magistrates to the Assizes. Ned Jarvis, an out-of-work labourer who had an obsessional hatred of those in authority, pleaded guilty to the murder of the Earl of Arkley when he was riding in the woods near his country home.

The prisoner also confessed to the murder of Lew Harrow, manager for the Estate of Mr. Quintus Tiverton, whose death had hitherto been unaccounted for.

The Earl of Arkley leaves a wife and three daughters. His heir, Mr. Quintus Tiverton, is believed to be travelling on the Continent and steps are being taken to notify him of his Uncle's death.

As Quintus Tiverton stopped speaking there was complete silence in the kitchen and then with a sigh that seemed to come from the very depths of his being, Jim said:

"That means, Sir, we can go home!"

"Yes, Jim, we can go home."

Putting the newspaper down on the table, Quintus turned and walked from the kitchen.

For a moment Selina could not move, and then automatically she put the pan containing the fish onto the stove and followed Quintus.

She found him standing in the centre of the Salon, staring into space as if he had no idea where he was or what he was doing.

She went to his side. Her hands went out towards him instinctively but she did not touch him; she only waited.

"I can hardly believe it!" he said after a moment.

There was silence again, and then in a very small voice Selina said:

"Now you have ... everything you want and are so ... important ... if you wish to be ... rid of me ... I shall understand."

She tried to speak calmly, but there was an unmistakable sob behind the words.

Quintus with a little laugh turned and put his arms round her.

"Can you really be saying anything so foolish?" he asked. "It is only that for the moment I feel I am a man who has been winded in a prize-fight. I am punch-drunk, my darling!"

He drew her closer and looked down into her anxious eyes.

"As Jim says, we can go home—home to a new life—a life I have always longed for—and, thank God, I need never touch a card again!"

"And you still ... want me?" Selina asked.

There was a very tender smile on Quintus's lips as he replied:

"Now at last, my precious, as your guardian, I can suggest a marriage of which I heartily approve."

His lips were very close to hers as he went on:

"Will you, beautiful Miss Selina Wade, marry not an impecunious gamester with nothing to offer you but his wits, but the very wealthy and eligible Earl of Arkley?"

He was laughing with happiness as he finished speaking, but Selina realised that he was waiting for her answer.

"I hardly know either of the gentlemen you describe," she murmured, "but I do wish to marry someone so wonderful, so kind, so noble that I know that without him life is unendurable, but with him it will be an ecstasy beyond words!"

"Oh, my sweet! My precious! My perfect little love!" Quintus cried.

He kissed her as she clung to him, and then as he raised his lips from hers he said:

"This has been my last gamble—a gamble with hearts—and I have won! God knows it is the greatest win that any gambler could desire!"

His voice seemed to ring out triumphantly round the small Salon as Selina moved from the circle of his arms.

"You still have to eat, My Lord!" she said with a hint of mischief in her eyes, "and breakfast is ready!"

"Then let us eat," Quintus replied, "for I have no wish to miss that train to Paris. I have a very important engagement there, as well you know!"

"Our wedding!" Selina smiled at him.

"Well, hurry up!" he said impatiently. "I want to make you my wife, and what could be a better reason for speed?"

Selina had reached the door while he was talking and now she looked back at him as he stood smiling in the centre of the Salon.

It seemed to her in that moment as if he had cast a burden from his shoulders and stood taller and even prouder than he had done before.

Her eyes lingered on him for a moment.

Then as if she could not help herself she ran towards him and flung herself into his ams.

"I love you . . . Oh, Quintus . . . I love you!" she

cried. "But when you get back to England will you be so grand that I shall . . . lose you?"

He sensed the anxiety behind the question and as he held her tightly against him he said:

"Have you forgotten that we belong to each other? By tomorrow night we shall be one person, Selina, and then there will be no escape, either for you or for me."

"That is all I . . . want," she whispered.

"The only thing to remember, my dearest heart, is that you are mine, now and for eternity."

Once again his lips were on hers, and they were enveloped with the divine, golden, scintillating happiness known only to those who win true love in the gamble of life.

ABOUT THE AUTHOR

BARBARA CARTLAND, the celebrated romantic author, historian, playwright, lecturer, political speaker and television personality, has now written over 150 books. Miss Cartland has had a number of historical books published and several biographical ones, including that of her brother, Major Ronald Cartland, who was the first Member of Parliament to be killed in the War. This book had a Foreword by Sir Winston Churchill.

In private life, Barbara Cartland, who is a Dame of the Order of St. John of Jerusalem, has fought for better conditions and salaries for Midwives and nurses. As President of the Royal College of Midwives (Hertfordshire Branch), she has been invested with the first Badge of Office ever given in Great Britain, which was subscribed to by the Midwives themselves. She has also championed the cause for old people and founded the first Romany Gypsy Camp in the world.

Barbara Cartland is deeply interested in Vitamin Therapy and is President of the British National Association for Health.

Barbara Cartland

The world's bestselling author of romantic fiction. Her stories are always captivating tales of intrigue, adventure and love.

☐	THE TEARS OF LOVE	2148	$1.25
☐	THE BORED BRIDEGROOM	6381	$1.25
☐	JOURNEY TO PARADISE	6383	$1.25
☐	THE PENNILESS PEER	6387	$1.25
☐	NO DARKNESS FOR LOVE	6427	$1.25
☐	THE LITTLE ADVENTURE	6428	$1.25
☐	THE SHADOW OF SIN	6430	$1.25
☐	LESSONS IN LOVE	6431	$1.25
☐	THE DARING DECEPTION	6435	$1.25
☐	CASTLE OF FEAR	8103	$1.25
☐	THE GLITTERING LIGHTS	8104	$1.25
☐	A SWORD TO THE HEART	8105	$1.25
☐	THE KARMA OF LOVE	8106	$1.25
☐	THE MAGNIFICENT MARRIAGE	8166	$1.25
☐	THE RUTHLESS RAKE	8240	$1.25
☐	THE DANGEROUS DANDY	8280	$1.25
☐	THE WICKED MARQUIS	8467	$1.25
☐	THE FRIGHTENED BRIDE	8780	$1.25
☐	THE FLAME IS LOVE	8887	$1.25

Buy them at your local bookseller or use this handy coupon: